A WIFE BY ACCIDENT

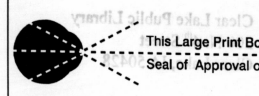

A WIFE BY ACCIDENT

VICTORIA ASHE

THORNDIKE PRESS

A part of Gale, Cengage Learning

GALE
CENGAGE Learning·

Detroit • New York • San Francisco • New Haven, Conn • Waterville, Maine • London

GALE
CENGAGE Learning®

LIBRARY OF CONGRESS CATALOGING-IN-PUBLICATION DATA

Ashe, Victoria.
    A wife by accident / by Victoria Ashe. — Large print ed.
      p. cm. — (Thorndike Press large print clean reads)
    ISBN-13: 978-1-4104-4379-3(hardcover)
    ISBN-10: 1-4104-4379-5(hardcover)
    1. Love stories. gsafd 2. Large type books. I. Title.
  PS3601.S534W54 2012
  813'.6—dc23   2011039177

Published in 2012 by arrangement with Black Lyon Publishing, LLC.

Printed in the United States of America
1 2 3 4 5 6 7 16 15 14 13 12

For Inspirations

CHAPTER ONE

"I hate my job." Hayely Black clenched her fist around a tangle of clothes hangers. She twirled the latest addition to her boss's considerable wardrobe out of the front seat and onto her arm.

"I hate my job," she repeated to herself as she struggled to balance a stack of oversized boxes on the other arm.

"And —" She paused and bumped the rickety car door shut with her hip. "I hate my job."

She couldn't even see to walk, much less put one foot in front of the other safely. She just knew if she fell and broke a leg carrying out Kathy L. Mark's errands, the woman would probably fire her for looking unprofessional with a cast that didn't match her skirt.

Hayely struggled with the boxes as a gust of wind threatened to knock them out of her hands. No, a year ago she would have never taken a job working for a woman like Kathy. But if she had to choose between putting up with the abuse to keep a steady paycheck or running back home with her tail between her legs — well, she couldn't even consider the latter.

With the packages precariously balanced, she took a few more baby steps, peered out from behind the stack, and moved cautiously forward. So far, so good. Now if she could just make it around the corner and inside to the elevator, someone in the office would no doubt see her and help.

Hayely took a step forward and then another, when the impact of something very large and hard slammed against her. The next thing she knew, the boxes went flying up, hitting her in the face as they fell. The force of whatever she'd just run into pushed her backward with the packages and she wobbled atop her high heels before finally catching her balance.

The overpriced clothing was still draped over her arm. Good. She breathed in deeply. At least she hadn't dropped that. She looked down at the ground in front of her. The lids on the boxes had held tight. This was her lucky day, she thought, and then her gaze froze.

A pair of well-worn, brown leather work

boots with rugged black soles caught her eye. The realization struck her that this was no wall she'd run into at all. Almost afraid to see who was wearing those boots, she tucked her chocolate-brown hair back behind her ear and slowly took in the crisp new jeans. Hayely's heart pounded furiously.

"I'm so sorry. It was an accident. I couldn't see you." She panicked and started to take a step back. She'd started to feel bad about plowing over some poor man until she saw the collision hadn't budged him an inch. A wall, she realized, would have experienced about the same level of damage.

He put his hands out with his palms facing her. "Don't —"

"Really, I didn't mean to."

Was he going to grab her? She'd heard about criminals targeting women who didn't look like they could get away quickly. And Kathy's boxes had ensured that. She took another step of retreat.

"— back up," he finished.

Horrified, Hayely looked down at her feet. Somehow her attacker theory began to slip away the second that awful grinding, popping noise sounded from under her shoe. She grimaced visibly.

"Not much for listening, are you?"

Hayely lifted her foot and stared blankly at the crushed pile of golden metal and glass on the pavement. "Think there's any chance a little superglue might do the trick?" She couldn't bring herself to look him in the face.

"That was a twelve-thousand-dollar watch."

Hayely's pulse raced. Twelve thousand dollars? That was almost half a year's salary to her. If she were the fainting kind, she'd have been flat on the ground next to the remains of the watch. The man's voice held a quiet rumble of power in it, as if when he used that tone there was no doubt he would talk his way into getting exactly what he wanted. His voice reminded her of a river, rushing deep and strong around boulders in its path, wearing them away slowly.

"You're kidding? You have insurance for it? I hope." She closed her eyes as he approached her. Please let him be insured.

"I just bought it five minutes ago. So, no. There's no insurance." He held out a receipt for an item that cost a sum with more zeros on the end than she cared to count.

Hayely opened her eyes and looked from the piece of paper up to his face. He didn't seem as angry as she would have been in his place. She checked to see if his lips were clenched together into a tight line. The way a man held his mouth could reveal his emotions — thank goodness this particular man's mouth still seemed relaxed. The corners of it even turned up just a bit. His hazel eyes didn't looked crazed with fury either, but he certainly wasn't letting her escape his narrowed gaze.

"And I knocked it out of your hand and stepped on it?"

He nodded.

"You didn't just drop it? It wasn't already broken?"

He shook his head the other way and crossed his arms over his plaid-shirted chest.

She ran her hand over her forehead and felt a tiny indentation where the corner of the box had found its mark. "Well, I don't know what to do about it."

He unfolded his arms. "You could try offering to pay me back for starters."

"Look, Mr. —"

"Tarleton. Gary Tarleton." He held out his hand to shake hers.

Hayely took his hand and was surprised his touch comforted her, finishing off her nagging fears of being mugged. In fact, her insides did a funny little flip-flop as she felt the warm skin and rough calluses brush against her fingers.

"I'm Hayely Black and there's no way on God's green earth I'll be able to pay that much money back. I just don't have those kinds of funds at my fingertips anymore."

"Don't you have a job?" Gary asked in a matter-of-fact tone.

"Ever see what an executive assistant makes?" she asked.

"You're a secretary then. Can't you get a higher paying job?" His arrogant expression told her it ought to be simple for her to just run out to the nearest company and take over the keys to the executive washroom.

"What do you think? I have exactly one month of work experience to my name, and I had to start somewhere."

She hadn't meant to run into him. She hadn't meant to break his watch. And he wanted to lecture her on career advancement? What was she? A magnet for people who wanted to launch into this subject? This guy would get along great with her father.

Gary scraped his hand across his rough, stubble-covered chin. "Monthly installments then."

Hayely shook her head and thought of the two-weeks-past-due electricity bill on her kitchen table. "My paycheck barely covers the bills. I have to eat, too, you know." Of course he didn't know. The man bought twelve-thousand-dollar watches.

"How about getting a loan?"

"No collateral," she countered.

"From a family member?"

"Definitely not."

If she ran back to her family for help with anything, her father would have her married to a wealthy old-money millionaire and registered for Harvard medical school before she could blink. She could hardly imagine anything she was less interested in.

"Do you have any better ideas then?" That gentle, gruff roll in his voice told Hayely that the man — Gary was still calm. Maybe twelve thousand dollars wasn't all that important to him after all.

Hayely shook her head miserably and her shoulder-length brown hair slipped out from behind her ears. "No. I'm all out of ideas."

Gary stood and scrutinized her for a moment. "In this job of yours, I assume you do some supply ordering, some shopping?" he finally asked.

"Yes. Why?"

He ignored her question. "How's your sense of style?" He surveyed her suit and saw that it matched her shoes, which was good enough for him. Her makeup was applied with some subtle class, too. He took that as a sign of good taste.

"I'm alright with colors and such, if that's what you mean."

"Are you responsible?"

"Usually. I mean, yes. Look, I don't want to get personal with you. I just want to figure out what I can do to make it up to you for breaking your watch."

Gary smirked, turning one corner of his mouth up just a little more. He ran his fingers through his already unruly brown hair. "You'll do."

"I'll do what?"

If he thought she'd trade her body for forgiveness of a debt, the Neanderthal had another thing coming. The way he was looking her up and down, it wouldn't surprise her if he suggested it.

Gary fell silent again. He walked over to her side and examined her hairstyle. Her sleek, unlayered hair and soft bangs gave her an air of simple sophistication. She kept herself in good shape and wore an understated suit that wouldn't draw any unwanted attention. He ran his hand over his dark stubble again as he looked back to her face.

"Nice features. Well spoken. Slight attitude, but he could overlook that," he said.

"Excuse me?"

14

"You'll definitely do. What I need is someone presentable, someone I'm not likely to become attracted to, though. Fewer complications that way. I can't afford any distractions for a while."

"Again — what?" Forget she'd just broken his precious watch. Hayely thought she had a perfect right to be angry now.

First this stranger, this irritating Gary Tarleton person, assessed her as if he were pricing livestock and then had the nerve to call her unattractive? She knew she was no supermodel, but she was a far cry from ugly. Where did he get off? She was about to tell him just what she thought of his personality when he spoke again.

"Here's the deal. I need two things in life right now — a temporary wife and an interior decorator. No questions asked. You'll have to furnish and fix up the inside of my new house from floor to ceiling and show up for a few meetings and dinners where I'll introduce you as Mrs. Tarleton. I don't want conversation. I don't want a friend. Just a business deal."

Hayely had no trouble meeting his gaze now. Was the man insane? She thought for a second that he was some desperate, middle-aged construction worker making a play for her. But what kind of construction worker could afford to plunk down twelve grand on a piece of jewelry?

Besides, after really looking at him, she could tell he wasn't more than a few years older than her — probably in his early thirties at best. He didn't have any wrinkles except for creases of scrutiny at the corners of his narrowed eyes, and only one or two grey hairs mixed in with that scruffy stubble of his. He might have been good-looking if his expression wasn't so terribly serious.

She took in a gulp of air. "Huh?" Disbelief blocked her words.

"I'm offering you a job. So you can pay off the watch."

Just a month ago Hayely had packed her bags, loaded up her car and started driving — all to avoid a life and a job someone else had picked out for her. But here she was, back between another devil and another deep blue sea.

"I got as far as you needing someone to decorate your house. That I could do. But marry you like that? That's not even legal, is it?"

Gary narrowed his sparkling hazel eyes at her again. "I'm talking about a six-month commitment at best. A contract arrangement, binding and legal. You can come over after work or on weekends. I don't care

16

when you work or how many hours it takes
to get the place finished. I just want it done
well. If it is, we'll call it even for the watch."

Six months? Hayely could feel the adrena-
lin surging through her blood. Could she
agree to something so bizarre? Six months
would buy back her independence, buy her
way out of this situation . . . Her family
didn't need to find out about the marriage
part, did they?

She raised her chin high to look at him
directly. "What if I don't agree?" There.
What would he say to that?

The corners of his mouth lifted up higher
— almost imperceptibly so, but definitely
higher. If she'd known who he was, he was
sure Hayely Black would have jumped at
the chance. Every other money-hungry
female in town would have, which was
exactly why he couldn't ask any of them.
Too many strings attached, too many complications.

"I'm glad you're so entertained," she said
when he didn't respond.

"Your eyes look like shiny smoke when
you get all emotional. Never seen pure grey
eyes before."

"Drop dead."

Gary shrugged his considerable shoulders
and hooked his thumbs into his pockets.

"We could always walk down to the police station. It's just a couple blocks away."

Hayely ran her hand across her forehead again and looked at the pile of pulverized watch. There was really no way she could imagine repairing the thing. The wind had already started to blow little bits of shattered glass and the watch's tiny inner workings across the parking lot. She cursed that husky, quiet voice of his. She'd walked right into his trap.

Gary tilted his head a little to the side. "Good. I'll take your silence as a yes. Do you have a business card?"

She fumbled inside her purse and handed him one of the company's little sticky notes with her office address on it. Writing her name and phone extension on it, she moved in slow motion as if she'd slipped into automatic pilot mode somewhere under his gaze. What was she doing? She simply couldn't see another way out of an expensive mess.

"I'll have someone courier over an agreement. Read it. Sign it."

He tucked her card into his shirt pocket with a frown and walked off across the parking lot with his big boots clunking on the pavement. He didn't even turn his head to look back.

■ ■ ■ ■

"I'm going to fire some idiot this week. I just haven't decided who yet." Kathy L. Mark stopped in front of Hayely's desk and tossed a thick envelope onto it. "Maybe it'll be someone who receives personal deliveries on company time."

With a saccharine smile she turned on her heel and walked off down the hall. Kathy always dressed in petite, tailored suits and worried openly about her thinning, anemic blonde hair, which she kept short enough to just brush the back of her neck. At sixty, she still fancied herself a traffic stopper. Hayely suspected that Kathy hadn't been any great beauty even in her prime.

Unkind thoughts were easy for her to have in that office. At least once a week, she and the rest of the staff suffered through Kathy's threats to fire one of them. Hayely looked daggers at Gary Tarleton's package, anonymously sent via a nearby law firm, on the desk in front of her. It had just turned her into Kathy's target of the week. It was Hayely's typical luck that the ever-hostile woman had happened to walk through the reception area just as the courier arrived.

Hayely's workday had ended at five

19

o'clock and it was already a quarter after. Did she dare leave so soon? She'd seen Kathy's wrath when an employee didn't donate an extra half an hour both morning and evening. But the envelope screamed to be opened. She thought she could actually feel it speaking to her fingertips.

Hayely scooped up her coat and purse, and had barely gotten into the elevator before she tore open the package. A local attorney had drawn up the paperwork and it all looked very legal and straightforward. Could she actually sign it? If she did, a strange situation would become frighteningly official.

She finished reading the document in her car and froze when she got to the last page. Gary Tarleton had drawn up the agreement exactly as he'd said except for that last paragraph. With unsteady fingers, she turned off her car radio so she could concentrate.

"An extra ten thousand dollars?" Her hands started shaking as she reached deep into the envelope and retrieved the key to Gary Tarleton's house. "Oh, Lord have mercy. He's added a bonus."

With that much money she could maintain her independence, resign from K. L. Mark Enterprises, and actually find a job she enjoyed. Who knew? Maybe she was fated to become an interior designer and this was the universe's way of showing her. And all it would take was six months of acting like Gary Tarleton's wife. How bad could that really be?

With a tremble, she took a roller ball pen from her purse and signed her name plain as day in indelible blue ink.

CHAPTER TWO

Hayely put the key Gary had sent her into the lock of his front door. She didn't think anyone was home yet — the place was far too quiet. She'd driven around the block several times before finally working up the courage to turn into his long, winding driveway.

The address matched the one on the note he'd sent, but she must have made a mistake somewhere along the line. This creation of light grey stonework and colorful stained glass wasn't a house; it came closer to being a castle, one with so much land behind it that she knew she was entering a kingdom.

Hayely walked up the grand cement stairs and gave the key a firm twist. To her amazement, the big wooden doors yawned open at her touch. She walked in and shut the doors behind her with a thud and click that echoed through the empty foyer.

"Anybody home?" she called and was

greeted only with the sound of her own voice coming back to her. She wondered where anyone who lived in a place like this usually went on a Saturday morning. Probably on a jet tour of Europe, she supposed.

There wasn't a stick of furniture as far as she could see. An enormous staircase spiraled upward in front of her and the marble floor of the entryway made her afraid to step on it. There wasn't so much as a throw rug or a leafy green houseplant to decorate the place. She kicked her shoes off to the side. She hoped more than anything that she wouldn't be expected to do all the housekeeping, too.

"It's no wonder he needed a decorator," she whispered to herself as she craned her neck back to look up at the high ceiling.

"It's high time, too. The place has been empty a couple of months now. We'd both like to stop eating off of cardboard boxes."

"I didn't think anyone was here." Her hand flew to her chest. She turned to see a slender man with striking auburn hair leaning against the wall underneath one of the massive stained glass windows. He gave her a pleasant smile, a genuine greeting without hesitation.

"I'm Charlie," he said as he shook her hand. "I sort of help Gary out with things.

23

He told me to expect you. The uh — minister should be here any time now. Guess I'm the witness, huh?"

Hayely swallowed hard. "I imagine it's better just to get it over with." She reminded herself that she had entered a business deal — a very lucrative one if she could just get through the next few minutes. She shook her head at her own thoughts. What had she expected anyway? Flowers, gifts and a reception? A honeymoon with champagne and chocolates? Not in her lifetime, she'd bet. And especially not in this strange situation she'd managed to get herself into.

Charlie looked at her with sympathy. "I tried to talk him out of this, but it's really the only way we could come up with."

"The only way for what? I know why I'm here. I just don't know why he is. I don't even know who he is for that matter."

"You don't know who Gary Tarleton is? Don't you ever read a newspaper or turn on the local news?"

A peculiar twist caught Hayely's insides. Maybe she was biting off more than she could chew. She could live on macaroni and cheese, have the telephone turned off, sell those diamond earrings she'd gotten three birthdays ago — she might be able to make monthly payments that way.

24

"I just moved here to Nevada a few weeks ago. Am I supposed to know who he is?"

Charlie studied her for a moment and made a surprised sound high in his throat. "No, I guess not."

They turned toward the sound of the front door opening again. Hayely hadn't seen Gary since the unfortunate incident with the watch, and maybe her panic and embarrassment had clouded her first impression of him. He was a larger man than she'd remembered. Tall and confident, he had the kind of smooth muscles earned from hard, honest work rather than evenings spent at a gym. The difference was easy to tell — her father had tried to set her up with enough card-carrying gym members.

Gary wiped his hands off on his already dirty jeans and tucked in his white T-shirt. Her first thought that he was a construction worker sprung to mind again. He was certainly looking the part right about then. If it was possible, his chin was covered with even more stubble than before. Hayely couldn't believe a man would grow a beard that looked that unkempt on purpose. He even had dust on his eyelashes.

"Got delayed at the Turner site." He turned a guarded expression toward Hayely and smiled wryly. She'd worn a casual white cotton dress that was buttoned tightly from the neckline and continued in a row of buttons all the way around her narrow waist. The demurely flowing skirt fell to her ankles.

His gaze rested on her pretty face. "At least you look the part of the bride. Good. Best to be believable."

A small, balding man with rounded glasses appeared in the doorway behind Gary. "I was so surprised to get Mr. Tarleton's call," he said. "Such an honor to be asked into your home. Ah, you must be the future Mrs. Tarleton."

The minister crossed the floor to Hayely and took both of her hands in his. "You're lovely. Just lovely. It's no wonder he wanted to snap you up so quickly. Are you ready to begin the ceremony?"

What had she gotten herself into? This was too much. Vows? She'd hoped to bypass the formalities and just sign the marriage certificate. She wasn't sure she could choke out wedding vows to this man she'd really only just met. Monthly payments. Somehow she'd scrape by and figure out a way to send him something each month. Something. Anything. Even it if took twenty years to pay him off.

■ ■ ■ ■

Gary narrowed his eyes as he watched Hayely freeze on the spot. The girl was absolutely terrified, he realized. Every muscle in her body had visibly stiffened. He shouldn't have put her in this position. She wasn't a money-driven corporate shark built to handle this sort of deal. For a moment he toyed with letting her off the hook.

He studied her soft, pretty face and white dress. No, he needed someone exactly like her in this role. There was no way around it. This arrangement was the only way he could keep the promise he'd made years and years ago, and Gary Tarleton always kept his word regardless of the cost.

He walked over and put his heavy arm around her small shoulders and gave her a quick squeeze. "She's a little nervous. Why don't we begin now?" he suggested.

The minister smiled and frowned ever so slightly. "Don't you want to change clothes first?" He pushed his round glasses up higher on his nose only to have them slip down again as soon as he moved his hand away.

Gary shook his head. "We'd better start with the 'I do's' now, I think." He stood at her side and smiled innocently at the minister. Just get it done with already.

Hayely leaned in closer to him. Her warm body felt good there, made him feel like he could give her all things secure and safe. She looked so small beside him that he had no doubt he could catch and hold her with one hand if her knees gave way.

She didn't look any more alert than a zombie as her lips formed a promise of marriage. He knew she could scarcely believe the sounds were coming from her own mouth. He couldn't believe it either. The world blurred and then cleared when Gary took her hand in his and slipped the wedding ring onto her trembling finger.

What sorts of lightning bolts would God use to strike him down for this? he wondered.

She held out her hand and stared at the platinum band looped with shiny diamonds, and all at once it was as if her senses came sailing back to her. She touched the ring gingerly and jumped as if the metal had shocked her, but then Gary slid his hand over hers again.

"You may kiss the bride," the minister finished.

Gary turned Hayely around to him, tucked his finger underneath her chin and raised her face to his. Darn if she wasn't prettier than he remembered. Those glossy grey eyes full of fear and uncertainty made him want to gather her into his arms and apologize for ever meeting her. But Hayely came complete with other distractions that interested him more at the moment. Her red rose petal lips begged to be kissed and he lowered his mouth dutifully to hers.

Hayely wasn't prepared for the jolt that leapt through her body. She'd been kissed before, longer and more passionately than this and by men she'd actually known for more than a few days. But this kiss, this delicate brush of Gary Tarleton's lips against hers, sent a shock through her. Consorting with the enemy, came the sudden thought.

"I'll see my way out," the minister said as he pushed his little round glasses higher up on his nose for the second time. "I can see you two want to be alone."

"You do that," Gary answered without breaking the contact his gaze had found with Hayely's. Her lips were only inches away. If he wanted to, he had the perfect excuse to kiss her again before she slipped away into business partner status again.

Hayely waited until the man with his little round glasses had disappeared through the doorway before she took a step back from Gary.

"What exactly was that supposed to be?"

Gary's eyebrows rose at the angry tone in her voice. "It's traditional to kiss the bride. The minister would have wondered if we hadn't."

"Well, my lips weren't part of the deal."

"A believable, make-believe wife is," he countered with a lopsided grin.

"Yeah? And how believable is a groom with three days worth of stubble and a T-shirt?"

"Charlie'll show you the ropes," he called as he turned and walked abruptly out of the house.

Hayely felt something akin to bewilderment as Gary left. Downright rude. That's what he was. One minute he was kissing her, the next minute annoying her — and then suddenly she was watching the door shut directly behind the seat of his jeans.

Charlie rested his hand on her shoulder and brought her back to the present. "Ready to get to work?" he asked.

She nodded. "I think that would be best."

"Great." Charlie smiled. "Let's start with the tour."

Charlie led Hayely around the first floor of the mansion. She lost count of how many rooms there were, but she distinctly remembered an exercise room, library with shelves built from floor to ceiling, an amazing blue-tiled indoor swimming pool, and a kitchen loaded with shiny, copper-colored appliances that any world-class chef would drool over . . .

They took the winding staircase to the second floor where Charlie said the bedrooms and bathrooms were. Every word he spoke echoed back to them. Gary's room, an enormous master bedroom, had only a mattress placed flat on the floor, but the possibilities were endless.

Hayely could imagine a set of gossamer, cream-colored curtains flowing against the ornate glass doors that opened up onto a high balcony. Not too frilly, but not so masculine as to weigh down the atmosphere. The adjoining bathroom with its round black marble tub was distinctly male, though. It screamed for thick terrycloth towels with a GT monogram embroidered in gold at their ends. She knew just where to buy those.

"So what do you think?" Charlie asked with an eager tone in his voice.

"I think I'm going to have the best time decorating this place. What's my budget?" For the first moment in the past few months, she was actually looking forward to something in her life. It was enough to almost push the earlier part of the morning out of her mind for a time.

"Budget?" Charlie laughed out loud. "There is no budget. Gary has accounts everywhere with your name already added to them." He handed her a credit card, which also had her name on it in metallic raised letters. "There's no credit limit on this one. Gary wants only the best in this house."

"That could cost an arm and a leg and probably the other leg, too." Hayely couldn't take her eyes off the credit card. She'd expected to see her last name, Black, imprinted there. But instead it read clear as crystal: "Hayely Tarleton." It seemed Gary had thought of every detail to make the charade seem real to the outside world.

"How did he get the credit card so fast?"

Charlie smiled at her. "You really don't have a clue who Gary Tarleton is, do you?"

"Oh, I'm getting a hint. But I'm also starting to get the feeling I have some research to do." She looked in awe up to the high ceiling as she stepped back down the staircase. Whoever he was, he apparently carved out a comfortable living for himself. His house was straight out of one of those fantasy home shows on cable television.

"Gary says that if you can't find exactly the right furniture locally, you should feel free to travel or buy it off the Internet. You have complete creative freedom. Gary is the master of delegation. I think it's one of the secrets of his success — that he just instinctively knows what people are good at. Take me for example. When we met almost twenty years ago in the —"

Charlie had definitely piqued Hayely's curiosity. "In the what?" she asked, urging him to continue. She just might start her research on Gary right then and there with Charlie.

Charlie waved his hand dismissively. "Never mind. I've said too much already and it's not my place to give away Gary's secrets. Just know that he's a good man, and he always honors his deals."

"Is he always so aloof? He's barely said two words to me since I smashed his watch. And I have to wonder what kind of man feels comfortable with an arrangement like we have now."

Charlie looked at her quizzically. He was used to women asking how much Gary's fortune was really worth or what he desired in a woman so that they could mold themselves into whatever description Charlie

33

gave. He'd had quite a good laugh watching reactions to whatever wild tale he created in a moment of humor.

Once he'd told someone that Gary loved to see women wear pink, and for the longest time that was the only color any eligible female in town would wear. Little did they know that Gary hated the "foofy" color. But never once over the years had any of them asked anything personal about Gary, and never once had any of them looked as openly sincere as Hayely Black. Would that change after she found out more about Gary?

"Don't take it personally," he finally said. "Gary watches people. Don't mistake silence for lack of interest. He's quite the charmer once he gets to know someone."

"And how much time does that usually take? To get to know him, I mean." The thought of tiptoeing on eggshells around Gary Tarleton for six months wasn't something Hayely thought she could endure without at least trying to learn something of the man. Her friendly nature would get in the way.

"Honestly?" Charlie asked. "I don't think you'd be able to do it within your six months. Then again you might. Who really knows the dark mind of Gary Tarleton?" He chuckled to himself.

"Well, I suppose I'll have to give up on the idea of friendliness then. But, for the sake of the show, you'd better give me some basics. For starters, what's his usual schedule? I'd like to know when to be out of the way."

"He works pretty much every day. He's up at sunrise and home late. But you have a key, so come and go as you please."

"Does he have any favorites? Colors? Furniture styles? Fabrics?" Hayely was at a loss. How could she decorate a mansion when she didn't even know the owner's taste? Then again, she wasn't even sure she could do the job in the first place. She was an executive assistant with a college degree she'd never put to use if she could help it.

"I don't think he'd take the time to care about most of those things. Except, I'd avoid pink if I were you."

"Ok, no pink then. Can you at least tell me which room he uses the most?"

Charlie's blue eyes lighted up. "That one I can answer. His den. He spends a lot of time there."

"That would be the room with the card table and a folding chair?"

Charlie nodded with a grin.

"Then that's where I'll begin."

Hayely smiled brilliantly. She couldn't wait to get started on her newfound project. She'd just received an exclusive catalog in the mail from one of the finest furniture makers in Vermont, a store her mother used to frequent. Would they ship all the way to Nevada? There was only one way to find out.

Hayely's Sunday couldn't have begun better. Already she'd placed an extravagant furniture order for Gary's den. With enough exquisitely carved mahogany and leather to fill the room, she couldn't wait for the shipment to arrive. She hadn't actually seen Gary since the day before when they'd finalized their agreement — she couldn't bring herself to think of it as her wedding day.

With paintbrush in hand, she stretched high on the ladder to reach the top corner of the den wall near the empty bookshelves. She'd chosen a shade of blue that would have been royal if it hadn't been subdued with just enough grey to keep it classy. The tones would lend themselves well to the rich, warm woods of the furniture that was scheduled to arrive in the middle of the week.

With each stroke of the brush, her mind drifted back more insistently to that single, soft kiss. The memory of it made her sigh out loud. Lord, if that's what the man could cause in her with a polite semi-kiss, what damage could he do if he really tried? What damage could he do if she actually liked him?

Gary kicked off his work boots at the front door and stepped quietly across the foyer as he approached the light-filled entrance to his office. The sleepy yellow glow from a chandelier that hadn't been there before made him smile. He'd expected the woman to do the job, but he hadn't thought she'd start right in the next morning. A good work ethic was something he could always appreciate. For once, he was glad he'd left work earlier than usual.

Hayely stretched up as tall as she could, leaning forward into the ladder as she put some final dabs of paint on the wall. Gary remained quiet with his hands in his pockets. He'd been wrong when he'd thought she wasn't pretty enough to draw unwanted attention. From what he could see, she was nothing short of beautiful in her worn jeans and T-shirt. The sedate dresses he'd seen her in before hadn't come close to doing her justice.

Her smooth, slender arms moved in gentle

waves across the wall, looking so feminine and graceful that he had to watch, and then watch some more. That song had said something about never making a pretty woman your wife, and Gary wished he'd remembered those lyrics before now. He felt guilty enough for luring her into the situation as it was, but to add physical attraction to the mix simply wasn't acceptable. He had other female employees; this one should be no different.

As she dropped the brush and stepped off the ladder, Hayely's hand fluttered to her chest the way he noticed it often did when she was startled. "How long have you been standing there?" The shock added a little splash of color to her cheeks. He liked it.

"Long enough."

Hayely took a moment to gather her wits as best she could. She composed herself quickly. He liked that, too.

"Your eyes get green when you're thinking evil thoughts."

He raised an eyebrow at her.

"I stocked your bathroom with soaps and towels today. I thought you might want a hot shower after work."

Gary walked across the room and picked up the fallen paintbrush from its place on the newspaper-covered floor. He reached his arm around her.

"You missed a spot."

"Thank you," was all she said.

Gary handed the brush back to her. She pulled her hand back quickly and almost dropped the brush again when his finger accidentally touched hers.

Gary pondered the expression in her eyes. She wasn't flirting, wasn't fawning over him, but of course she wouldn't — she didn't even know the magnitude of his wealth if what Charlie said was right. She knew he owned an impressive house, was fairly well off and had cornered her into doing exactly what he wanted. Something other than attraction might turn those eyes of hers into shining silver that reflected his own face back to him. Maybe what he saw there was actually open dislike. Or fear. After all, he'd been tyrant enough to insist on an arrangement she couldn't possibly enjoy.

"Could we talk for a minute?" she asked, growing visibly uncomfortable under his scrutiny.

He conceded with a nod. He wasn't big on small talk, but he owed her in some way, didn't he?

"I know I froze during the ceremony," she said. "But I just wanted you to know that I intend on living up to my end of the bargain."

"I know. From the looks of things, you're doing an excellent job of it. I wouldn't have thought of using blue in here. And Charlie mentioned something about a furniture shipment coming in a couple days." He cleared his throat.

Hayely looked at him for a moment, blinked and nodded. "I was thinking of doing the kitchen and your bedroom next," she said at last.

Gary nodded his approval. "Whatever you like. I think I mentioned you might need to be here during a couple dinner parties, too. After the décor is in place."

Hayely tucked her glossy hair back behind her ears. "I was meaning to ask you about that. Obviously, I'm keeping our arrangement from my family. And I'm not saying a word at work either. But, what if someone starts talking or if we have to be seen together somewhere public? I don't know what you do for a living, but I get the impression people around here seem to know you."

"Ah." Gary smiled — flashed what he thought was his best smile in fact.

"My father would kill me and I'd probably get fired if people at my office found out."

"Fired for getting married?"

"You don't know my boss. Kathy Mark fires people for breathing wrong."

Gary had recognized the company name on Hayely's sticky note and the truth was, he did know Kathy Mark. He'd met her a year or so ago at some local event and she'd persistently tried to get him to toss some business toward her little company ever since. He hadn't given her much thought after instructing his executive assistant to answer all K. L. Mark correspondence with polite refusals, but it grated on him whenever he saw someone in authority mistreat people. He'd heard the rumors.

"Well," he said, "I don't anticipate many nights out on the town for us. Low key is the plan." He might have to rethink that plan. She really was pretty. He wouldn't mind seeing her dressed to the hilt with her hair swept up off her neck and diamonds dripping off her earlobes. Maybe a few nights out with his new wife wouldn't be such a bad idea.

"Don't get any wild ideas about staying in either," Hayely countered. "I'm sure women fall at your feet. You'll have to find one of them if you want — that."

41

"Believe me. I'm strictly business." But his eyes never wavered from her.

Hayely's hand flew to her throat. Flushed. Conspicuous.

"You look more and more like a mountain man every time I see you."

So maybe he ought to think about trimming his mop of wavy brown hair and maybe even take a razor to some of that stubble. He ran one hand over his square chin.

"You might have a point."

"I think I'll call it quits for the day if you don't mind. I've got to get up early for work in the morning," she said.

When she got near him, Gary almost reluctantly turned to let her pass. A nagging thought pressed at him, one he hadn't considered before. It wouldn't seem right for her to be leaving the house just as darkness fell each day. Someone, some neighbor, would eventually notice the pattern. His worries were sidetracked as a whiff of vanilla and chocolate caught his attention.

"Did you bake something?" He frowned and then smiled. No one had ever cooked in the big, empty house before. It made the place feel homey.

Hayely shrugged nonchalantly on her way out. "I made chocolate chip cookies. They're on a plate in the kitchen. Tomorrow I'm stocking up all the cupboards. People could starve to death around here."

With a smile and a sigh she shut the heavy front doors behind her.

As soon as her car sputtered out of the driveway, Gary made a lumbering dash for the kitchen. He couldn't remember the last time he'd eaten hot, homemade chocolate chip cookies. Having a pretend wife had more advantages than he'd imaged — and he'd discovered a few more of them in one evening.

CHAPTER THREE

At exactly quarter till eight in the morning, Hayely was already at her desk typing up a memo for Kathy when the woman herself walked by. With her hands hidden under her desk, Hayely quickly slipped the wedding band off her finger and into her purse. She felt ridiculous wearing it anyway.

"Hayely," she greeted without looking directly at her. Instead, her boss glanced at the clock and then briefly at Hayely's desk before walking off down the hall.

"Good morning." Hayely felt the muscles in her neck and shoulders constrict. She could tell what kind of mood Kathy was in just by watching the way she walked, as if she were on her way to a matter of such importance that she had no time for civilities.

Hayely had gotten to the office earlier than usual that morning so she could have her real work done in time to do a little research.

With the Internet a click away, she wanted to see what she could find out about Gary Tarleton. Who was he exactly? She brought up the online version of the local newspaper and typed his name into the box for searches.

And there it was. She'd sold herself to Nevada's very own version of Donald Trump, and all for twelve thousand dollars that he would hardly miss after what she'd gleaned from the article. Not that the amount mattered, she cautioned herself. She'd broken that watch and it was her responsibility to pay for it.

But still, Gary could have hired the best interior designer on the planet and rented a supermodel to pose as his wife for half a year. Why on earth would he want her? She gritted her teeth as the answer came: because she could be bought cheap and she owed him.

Apparently, Mr. Gary Tarleton owned a number of architectural, engineering and construction firms all under the umbrella of his enormous local parent company — not to mention considerable stock in several large corporations and membership in all sorts of organizations. The man was a tycoon!

No wonder Charlie had laughed at her

uninformed comments. And no wonder Gary looked like a construction worker. He probably went down to one of his company's sites from time to time and wanted to fit in with the crew.

Hayely clicked on another link. "Wow," she said aloud.

In front of her was a picture of Gary she would never have imagined. Dressed to kill in a tuxedo, clean-shaven and with closely cropped hair, he was something closer to James Bond than the mountain man he'd resembled the day before. She peered closer at the picture.

All the people standing in the background behind him faded before her eyes as one person came into focus. Kathy L. Mark. What were the odds her boss did business with her new husband? No, she would have seen some trace of that in all the papers that floated across her desk. But it was obvious Kathy at least knew who Gary was.

Hayely shut down her Internet browser and a few seconds later an e-mail notice popped up on her screen. Kathy had written, "You need to tell me your work schedule. I believe you are to start at eight A.M., but it was well past that when you arrived today. Please advise."

Hayely's blood ran cold. She knew what

this was. She'd seen Kathy use the same method on a marketing assistant who had resigned in tears just the week before. The woman was creating a false documentation trail to build a case for firing her. Of course, Kathy's preferred outcome was to frustrate Hayely into quitting. Less legal hassle that way. What had she done to raise her boss's ire so soon? She could only begin to imagine.

With a dry lump in her throat, Hayely typed, "My schedule is still eight to five. When we greeted each other this morning at 7:45 A.M., I assumed this was acceptable. Please let me know if you would like me to arrive earlier and I can adjust my schedule."

Even as she hit the send button, she knew her reply wouldn't find its way into her personnel file the way Kathy's initial accusatory e-mail would.

With her bills stacking up on the kitchen table, Hayely had to survive at K. L. Mark Enterprises just five and a half more months. Smoothing the front of her skirt, she stood and began down the hall toward Kathy's office to sort things out. If she'd learned anything, it was that her boss preened under flattery like none other and maybe she could buy her job a little more time that way even though it turned her

47

stomach.

As she walked to the end of the hall, hushed voices just around the corner stopped her in her tracks. Someone was talking about her, and not even the tone of voice was flattering.

"And did you see what that Hayely idiot had on today?" Kathy's voice hissed. "She looks like she dresses straight out of a thrift store. I'd die before being seen that way."

Hayely recognized the other female voice as that of the chief financial officer, one of a couple piranhas Kathy kept near her for support.

"I know. That shirt looks like a man's. Good thing she's not sitting up at the front where people can see her — not that the new receptionist looks any better. I don't think she's going to work out any better than the last two."

Hayely had heard enough. She wished she could sail around the corner with her head held high, tell the two catty women what she thought of them and quit on the spot. But she couldn't.

She'd summoned a large dose of rebellious energy a month ago when she'd told her father she was moving out of the house and not entering medical school as he wished. She hated to get involved in another conflict, have another confrontation so soon after that fiasco. Besides, when she'd talked to her father, she'd at least known what she wanted. But what did she want now? A little basic on-the-job respect would be a good place to start.

Her cheeks flushed heated crimson under the insults she'd just overheard. In spite of Gary's etiquette shortcomings, he had been impressed enough with her taste to hire her. Now she wasn't sure if that was a compliment or not. But she could at least bet Gary never doubted what he wanted. He seemed to know exactly how to get from point A to point B. Better yet, he knew what his point B was. Hayely thought she might take a page from his book when her six months were up.

Even if she didn't have to work for Kathy to pay the bills, where would she work? Life with her bottom in a chair behind a word processor didn't suit her. The complete lack of creativity bored her to tears.

She didn't quite think she was built to be a construction worker, either. She smiled to herself. Not like Gary was built. She breathed in and out, letting the urge to confront Kathy pass.

The hours limped by in agony before it was time for Hayely to leave the office. She breathed an enormous sigh of relief and drove straight for Gary's house. She'd put in several more large, expensive furniture orders during her lunch break and wanted to get some more painting done before it all arrived. She could decorate the house easily in the given time frame and was surprised at how she enjoyed it. She loved the way her mind could wander into memories and ideas while she painted.

She walked in through a side door and headed for the kitchen after kicking her shoes off along the way. No sooner than she'd stepped through the door, the refrigerated delivery truck from the grocery store pulled into the driveway. Perfect timing, she thought with a smile.

Bag after bag, the driver carried the groceries inside. The kitchen floor was soon heaped with crackling brown paper bags and soft white plastic ones. She didn't know what sorts of food Gary might like, but she knew what she preferred. And, after all, Charlie had told her to do whatever she liked.

In the corner below some cabinets, Gary had built in something of a closet lined with cool cement. Hayely smiled. This was the equivalent of a root cellar brought indoors. She loaded it up with bottles of wine and bags of potatoes and onions. These things would stay just the right temperature there, she guessed.

She turned and opened up one of the shiny double doors of the copper-faced refrigerator. Hayely whistled low. She could fit enough food in there to feed a small country. The bags of fresh fruit and vegetables were quickly stored away in the gold-labeled glass drawers inside.

Next she looked at the big bags of flour, corn meal, sugar, powdered milk and a variety of other gourmet baking essentials. They would fit perfectly in one of the lower cabinets. And then there were the canned goods . . .

In less than an hour, Hayely had a kitchen stocked full of all the foods she thought a kitchen should have. Then she began to make dinner. Days were growing longer as spring neared, but at last the sunlight had begun to fade for the evening.

She set some potatoes to boil. The house seemed strangely lonely and far too quiet without Gary there. Of course, he didn't talk much when he was there. But still, she almost hoped he would come home early just to give her something to take her mind off the lousy day she'd had.

"Home? What a stupid word to even

think," she said aloud to herself. This wasn't her home. She shouldn't kid herself for a second about that. No sense getting too cozy. As soon as the six months were up, Gary would give her that promised ten-thousand-dollar bonus and send her on her not-so-merry way back to the small apartment that really was her home.

Gary stood inside the foyer and grinned when he saw Hayely's shoes kicked off in the corner. She was always so timid about scuffing the marble floor. He should have designed a log cabin with floors people could track dirt in on, but the architectural artist in him had gotten carried away and designed the house he'd pictured in fairy tales. He unlaced his big work boots and set them down beside her little black pumps.

An amazing, heavenly smell drifted to him as he lined up his boots. These were not the usual smells of paint and plaster; this was the aroma of a good old-fashioned home cooked meal. How many years had it been since he'd had one of those? He couldn't even remember.

He walked into the kitchen and plunked himself down wearily at the table. Hayely heaped his plate full of food and smiled at him. His nose had a black smudge on it and there was a ragged tear above the pocket on one of his white T-shirts.

"You shaved," she noticed. Her gaze scanned the planes of his face and he saw her hands tremble just so slightly.

He looked up at her with curiosity as she set a bowl full of mashed potatoes, a platter of asparagus wrapped in bacon, and another dish of poached salmon down in front of him.

"You don't have to cook for me, you know. That wasn't part of the deal." He gazed up at her and thought he caught something wistful in her expression.

Hayely stood next to him. "I don't mind. It's nice to be able to do something that someone else appreciates. Especially after eight long hours at that office."

He took a huge fork full of fluffy potatoes and gulped them down. "I was getting sick of fast food. And I can't cook worth a darn." He shoveled in more potatoes after swirling in some more butter.

"Well, I'm glad you're happy. I'll be painting the living room if you need anything." She started to walk around him when he caught her.

His fingers closed gently around her wrist. "You're not going to eat?" he asked with only the faintest hint of disappointment and then quickly resumed his former manner.

"You'd want me to? With you, I mean?" She looked from his green-brown eyes to his hand at her wrist.

"Absolutely." He released his loose hold and gestured brusquely to the seat across from him. "I'd like to talk with you."

"You would? I didn't think you'd want to converse with the hired help." The gleam in her eyes showed that she teased.

He nodded and swallowed his food. "Why wouldn't I? We all have to suffer through meetings sometimes. You're not the exception."

She sat down and helped herself to some asparagus. "You told me you didn't want conversation or questions."

He smiled wickedly. "You paid attention to that? I said a lot of things in that sentence I should amend."

"Well, you don't generally seem to be the talkative type. Anyway, it doesn't matter."

"What type do I seem?" he asked.

Hayely's hand shook again as she picked up her fork. "I didn't mean anything bad. We just haven't exactly spoken much."

He propped his muscular arm up on the tabletop. "I figure if I don't know a person or don't like a person, there's not really much need for small talk."

She rolled her head side to side and relaxed. "Guess I must have passed the test."

"This fish is delicious," he said with a sound of appreciation low in his throat. After a steady week of hamburgers and fast food tacos, a salmon dinner was just short of heaven. "Actually, I wanted to talk with you about something in specific."

"Okay."

"You need to move into this house with me," he declared with a casual shrug.

Hayely almost choked on her food and her eyes widened. His actions had already surprised her several times over. He alternated between setting her on edge with his insane demands and then soothing her with his low, calm voice.

But this? This was crazy talk.

"I'll hire someone to move your things into one of the empty bedrooms tomorrow," he continued. He waved his fork in the air as if in the grip of some great revelation. "Or even better — buy yourself new furniture for that room and sell your old things if you want. Or put them in storage. Whichever. I'll have the movers do what you want tomorrow while you're at work."

Hayely stared at him in dumbfounded silence. This was the second time she'd seen him genuinely expect the impossible to be done in the snap of a finger.

"Are you nuts?" she finally asked in the calmest tone she could muster.

Gary stopped chewing and looked up at her with the same self-assured expression she'd seen when she stepped on his watch.

"I made a promise when I was younger and I mean to keep it. I won't be able to keep it unless a particular man in a position of power allows me to. And he won't allow me to unless he sees I'm a family man with a stable home and a wife."

"I still don't understand why I have to move in," she said with a hint of stubborn confusion.

"Because I'll be contacting this man tomorrow and the minute I do, he'll start keeping a very close eye on me. And on you. If you come and go every evening and he catches wind of it, he'll know something's not right. I can't afford for him to suspect anything."

"This whole thing had better not be about some multi-million-dollar acquisition you promised yourself you'd chase down and conquer when you were younger."

"It's not," Gary said through clenched teeth. "And I don't think that's what you think of me either."

Hayely planted her elbow on the table and rested her forehead in the palm of her hand. "I have a one-year lease on my apartment. Ten months left to go."

"I'll pay it off."

She groaned. "What about my mail? My phone? I'll have to give the new information to my office and my family, too. What if someone calls and you answer the phone?"

"I'll give you a cell phone with your own private number tomorrow. I don't see a problem with the address change. No one will recognize it."

"Are you kidding? This is the most exclusive area of town." Gary's estate took up most of the area all on its own, she mused.

"Tell them you're house-sitting for a friend for a few months." He cut apart the last succulent piece of salmon.

Hayely leaned back in her chair. "You have an answer for everything, don't you?"

She knew he enjoyed the way her emotions swam so openly across her eyes when she was coming to an agreement. She'd never been able to help that.

"You'd never make a good corporate negotiator."

She sighed.

"Think of it this way, Mrs. Tarleton. You'll have something to put into a savings account now. You'll be saving all that rent money. Grocery, electricity, water and phone bill money, too. Look at me as your financial plan."

She waved her hands in the air. "And that. That's another thing." Laughter threatened to bubble up inside her. Incorrigible. That was the word she'd use to describe him. Incorrigible and slightly antisocial in an endearing way.

"That?"

"That 'Mrs. Tarleton' thing. It's on all the accounts and all the credit cards. I think I can avoid changing it on everything else. Lots of women keep their maiden names. And I've tried not to buy much locally, but I have to sign that new name for all the delivery men anyway, so I might as well just shop here. Everyone in this city is going to know we're married within the month at this rate."

"All the more reason for you to move in here by tomorrow. At least we've managed to keep it out of the papers. What does it really matter, though? If letting the secret out makes it more convincing, so be it. I kind of like the idea."

Hayely pushed herself away from the table, alternated between laughing and gritting her teeth, and finally stomped her foot down once. He was absolutely infuriating without even trying. She'd lose her job instantly and her family would disown her for sure, but he didn't seem to give that much thought at the moment.

"I'll be ruined! Don't you even care if I'm ruined?"

She rose up on the balls of her feet a little and then marched away from the table. Just as she passed Gary, he reached out and caught her arm again. This time he stood to face her.

Without a word, he caught her other wrist, gently guided her back around to face him, pulling her slightly closer to him in the process.

"Look up at me, Hayely," he commanded.

She turned her face up, meeting his gaze defiantly. "You know, I enjoy decorating your home. But I hate the circumstances of it."

"We signed a contract. What would you have me do?" he asked softly.

"Get a new homeowner's insurance policy that would have covered that stupid watch."

Gary dropped her hands and stepped away. He wasn't sure where the boundaries were. He'd paid for her services, and if he crossed any line she might feel — well, she might believe he looked at her without the respect she deserved and would hate him for it.

But he did respect her. He hadn't been able to get the way she spoke with such poised, calm fire out of his head for the last two days. He admired that quality in a woman. He also wondered how anyone as classically pretty as Hayely could come across so sure of herself yet so uncertain about everything around her at the same time.

They stood facing each other in silence for moments, unsure, breathing. The thud of the front door shook them both and the spell was broken.

"Charlie," Hayely greeted too enthusiastically. "Would you like some pineapple upside down cake?"

Was that relief or disappointment in the air between them?

Charlie crossed the room toward them, quickly closing the space with his long, skinny legs. "No one's fool enough to say no to that offer," he said.

As Charlie sat down, Gary nodded at him and then left the room.

"What's with him?" Charlie asked.

Hayely poured them both a cup of coffee to go with the cake. "We just had a discussion, that's all. Looks like I'm moving in

60

tomorrow."

Charlie looked from Hayely to the dirty dishes scattered across the table. "Did you two just eat dinner? And I missed out?"

Hayely nodded. "You'll have to come earlier next time. I got a new recipe book the other day."

Charlie shook his head. In the twenty years since he'd met Gary, the times they'd had to relax and eat a home-cooked meal had been few and far between. There had been too many business luncheons, too many airplane meals to count, too many well-meant setups with women who were mostly captivated by Gary's bankbook.

"Didn't you hear me say I'm moving in?" Hayely frowned at him. The man had seemed lost in his own world for a moment.

Charlie waved his hand cheerfully. "Oh, I already know about that. Gary was worried someone might see you leave. Then sure enough, our accountant was coming here last night and asked him why his wife was going out of town so soon after the wedding. Gary didn't want that kind of assumption to happen again."

"Oh." She took a sip of coffee and looked thoughtfully at Charlie. "Gary was just telling me about the promise he'd made — why he needed a temporary wife. It sounds awfully important to him."

Charlie assessed the casual look on her face carefully. If Gary trusted her, then he could. "Well, after growing up in that place, he knows firsthand what it's like. He wants to make sure those kids have the absolute best."

Hayely gazed into her coffee mug. If she pushed the subject, Charlie might realize how little she really knew and not let something slip later. And she didn't know when she might need to understand more about her new boss. Co-conspirator. Husband. Whatever he was to her.

"I'd better go upstairs and let Gary know which room to move my things into." She gave Charlie a smile and left him alone at the table with the entire cake and a fork.

She reached the top of the stairs and called out, "Gary? Are you up here?" Without much in the way of furniture, a cold museum-like echo came back her. "Gary?"

Gary heard her voice and stepped from his bedroom and walked toward the hall. He was just getting ready to take a shower and was still grinning because of the plush towels and new supply of toiletries he'd found in his bathroom. He'd mostly made due with his collection of miniature samples from hotels ever since the house's construction had wrapped up.

"I'm right here," he called out as he rounded the corner. Gary stood only a few feet away from her and ran his fingers through his hair.

Hayely said quietly, "I didn't mean to interrupt." She glanced down at the bar of bay rum soap in his hand. "Glad you found things. I didn't know which cabinet to put them in."

Gary felt himself smile again. "Why, Mrs. Tarleton, I had no idea you'd gone so far above and beyond the call of duty," he murmured. "Fancy soaps even."

"I'm just earning my bonus."

"The cooking alone would have done that."

"I cook because I enjoy it."

"Not because I do?" A smile played at the corner of his lips.

"It's a side-effect that couldn't be helped." Hayely smiled. Or at least threatened to.

"If you're wondering," Gary said, "I hope I'm keeping up my end of the bargain, too. I've been pleased — more than pleased with how you've held up yours. You've proven yourself to be an intelligent, attractive woman. You had a talent or two hidden away that I hadn't suspected and — I'm trying to say you're an asset."

A furrow crossed Hayely's brow and as such an "attractive woman" he worried she might make a snappy comeback about sexual harassment in the workplace. She looked with widened eyes at the man in front of her.

"You said I've 'proven' myself. But what was your first impression of me, Gary? I want the honest truth. Did you think I looked frumpy? Unattractive? Dimwitted?"

Gary's low laughter subsided into a chuckle as he ran his hand along his chin. "I didn't mean it that way. I've never seen any woman less frumpy. The day we met I wasn't thinking of anything other than a means to an end. It's inexcusable. I apologize."

Hayely's hand fluttered to her mouth. "No, I'm the one who's sorry. I don't know why I even let myself ask that. I shouldn't have. Bottled insecurities tend to push their container's cork skyrocketing at the strangest times."

Gary studied her eyes, full of a subsiding emotion that looked like splinters of crystal. He thought strangely about reaching out to smooth back her hair, then thought the better of it. She might take it the wrong way. There would be no right way to take it.

"It must have been bothering you," he said at length. "Whoever gave you the idea you were unattractive?"

"Something petty I overheard today. And all the things you said that day I ran into you."

"As I said, my mind was on my problems that day. Did I mention I'm often stupid and inept around women?" he asked with a low chuckle.

"This is a really inappropriate conversation," Hayely said with a start. "I think being in this house together makes things seem more casual than they are sometimes."

Gary nodded. "I'm sure that's it. But before we go back to strictly business, let me say this. Hayely, you look like a modern-day 1940s movie star without the ego. The way you dress, the way you carry yourself." He paused and looked at her expression closely. "That's all."

"I appreciate that you're trying to make me feel better." She closed her eyes as if some great tragedy had befallen her and then quickly opened them again.

"Don't mention it." Gary cleared his throat. "Now what can I do for you?"

"I wanted to ask about my room. You can move my things into whichever one you like. I have to tell you I'm hoping for one with a fireplace and a nice view of the grounds, though. Since I've got to live here, might as well make it good."

"You're not going to fight me on this?" he asked.

"What would be the point? You're the boss."

Gary watched until she disappeared down the winding staircase, her stocking feet making no noise at all. He shook his head silently.

He'd avoided complications that might interfere with his focus on the company like a contagious disease all his life. So how was it that he suddenly had a shopping, decorating, cooking, laughing woman living in his home? How was it that he'd become so bent on keeping a childhood promise that he'd blocked everything else from his mind? Still, he had to go through with the plan. He hoped Hayely understood and didn't loathe him for it.

"You're getting soft, Tarleton," he said to himself before he turned to go take that shower.

CHAPTER FOUR

Hayely had never considered it possible that she could be more miserable outside her father's house than in it. In the span of a month, she'd turned her life into a giant disaster and didn't know exactly how to go about correcting the situation.

She thought she might even be missing Gary some — probably caving in under the stress at work and the sheer emptiness of the big stone house while he was away. Charlie stopped by to check on her from time to time, but after a full week and then two had passed, she found herself straining her neck toward the door at every sound.

Soon after Gary had gone out of town, the much-anticipated shipment of furniture had arrived all the way from Vermont and Hayely couldn't wait to show it off.

The den looked like something from a hundred years ago with its heavy mahogany wood and rich brown leather. The desk and chair she'd chosen for Gary simply oozed understated power. A rug twisted with muted colors rested between the furniture legs and the hardwood floor below. With a painting of the English countryside she'd particularly liked and a plant or two, Hayely called that room complete and moved her efforts fully to the master bedroom.

When Gary returned he would find a giant bed with four posts carved of mahogany in the same style as his desk downstairs in the den. Those gauzy, cream-colored curtains she'd envisioned were in place, as was the rest of the bedroom furniture. She even painted the walls a dark cream and hung a large, medieval-looking tapestry full of reds and blues against one of them as a finishing touch.

Then her attention turned toward her own room. Why the movers had instructed her things delivered to the bedroom next to Gary's was beyond her. Surely he wouldn't have requested such an arrangement, but then, it was the second largest bedroom. The location was probably her fault — she realized it when she walked into the room. There in the corner was her own stone fireplace, just as she'd requested.

As night fell, she started a small fire and curled up in front of the hearth with a book.

She pulled her comforter off the bed and smoothed it out underneath her for some cushioning. Some thick, plush carpeting was definitely in order.

Hayely's mind wandered from the novel in her hand as she stared off into the hypnotic flames. What would she do with herself in just five months? If office work wasn't her calling, then what was? The only time she was truly content was when she was working in this house for Gary. But that would all end soon — too soon. Six months rang out like a harsh jail sentence at first, but now she almost dreaded the end of that time.

She was so absorbed in her thoughts and so very tired from the day's work that she didn't hear the sound of a car arriving in the winding driveway outside.

The yellow cab slipped through the rain and turned its wheels against the circular curb near the front door. Gary stepped out of the taxi, tipped the driver and pulled his luggage inside. From the silence that met him, he assumed Charlie had returned to his own house and Hayely was probably asleep upstairs.

"Anybody home?" He kept his voice low just in case.

Charlie rose from the kitchen table as his boss entered the room. "Good trip?"

Gary nodded and looked around the transformed kitchen and out into the formal dining room. "You really ought to just move in, too. You practically live here anyway." He paused and took in the changes around him. "She's made quite a bit of progress, hasn't she?"

Charlie nodded in return. "So what did Mr. Bellmark have to say?"

"He nearly confirmed that the children's home is up for sale. He has plans for it, but he hasn't confided in me what they are. It's hard to believe that the time has come already. Did you know he's almost eighty-years-old now?"

Charlie shook his head. "I haven't seen him in years. Seems like a lifetime ago. Any luck convincing him to let you buy it from him?"

Gary chuckled low in his throat. "I don't think he believed me when I told him I wasn't going to let anyone bulldoze the place."

"I wouldn't doubt it. You were just ten years old then."

Gary gave Charlie a surly look that told him he couldn't comprehend why his being a boy at the time should make a hair of difference.

Charlie smiled, stretching a few freckles across his cheeks. "Ah, I forget the great Gary Tarleton was never a mere boy."

"Absolutely right." Gary thrust his hands into his pockets. "But the stubborn old guy is staying true to his word, too. He says he'd rather see it demolished than let someone disreputable get his hands on it."

"Did you tell him about Hayely?"

"Of course. I made it a casual, personal visit. But Charlie, we're not even close to convincing him. You know, I didn't even have a picture of my own wife in my wallet to show him when he asked."

"This is getting complicated."

Gary ran his hand along a new five o'clock shadow. What he wanted of Hayely had ballooned far above his original intentions. There was no way they could hide their marriage from the public and make it convincing at the same time. Even a media campaign would be to his advantage. If he'd had a real wedding, he'd bet photographers would have been all over it. But whatever benefited him would probably hurt Hayely more, and after hearing what she'd said in the kitchen, he didn't want to make things worse if he could help it.

Gary smiled to himself. "I've got an assignment for you tomorrow, Charlie."

"Just say the word."

"I want you to go out and buy a black — no, a silver BMW. Get one of those really expensive retro-designed models with the red leather interior. If I know her taste, she'll like that."

"It's for Hayely? You like her, I think." Charlie grinned broadly.

"I couldn't stand to have a good employee seen in that mess, much less one who's supposed to be my wife. When I pulled into the driveway and saw her car parked there — the bumper is falling off, she's got the hood held down with a piece of wire, and every time she drives off to work it takes ten minutes for the exhaust cloud to leave. And did you see the patch of rust holding the trunk on? It's not even safe."

"So, in other words, you like her," he pressed.

Gary sighed. "Yeah. She's a good person."

"You're married to her. It wouldn't be all that hard to make the relationship —"

"Don't push your luck, Charlie." He shot his friend what was supposed to be a quelling look. "I'm off to bed."

Gary walked up the stairs, clunk after clunk. He'd forgotten to take his shoes off in the foyer and his boots weighed heavily with every step. Charlie was really rotten for bringing up the subject. The more he got to know Hayely, the guiltier he felt about their contract. And now Charlie had put ideas into head that had no business being there.

The door to her room was most of the way open in front of him, so he placed his hand flat against it and pushed it back farther. Hayely was stretched out on her side in front of the red glow of the dying embers covering the bottom of her fireplace. From the way her head was rested against one outstretched arm, Gary knew she'd fallen asleep.

Oh so quietly, he tugged another blanket off of her bed and stretched it out over her. As he tiptoed from the room, her drowsily slurred voice stopped him.

"You're home," she said. "I didn't hear you come in."

"I didn't mean to wake you," he answered softly.

Hayely sat up underneath the blanket. "You don't need to whisper. I'm already awake."

Gary walked back to her and sat down with her on the floor. Her face, softened by sleep, was flushed from the heat of the fire and just looking at her stirred something protective inside him.

"Did you have a good trip?"

"Yes and no. I met with the man I told you about — Mr. Bellmark."

"Ah. The one holding the power over your promise."

"That would be him, yes. I'm afraid our work might be for nothing. Our ruse isn't fooling him a bit," Gary said with a shake of his head.

"What happened?"

"The cagey old buzzard asked to see a wedding picture, and I didn't have one in my wallet. Most husbands would."

"I see."

"Hayely, this isn't going to work. With our current arrangement, he's never going to believe we've created a home together. I can't ask any more of you than you've already given."

"I know what I said. But I was angry and a little stunned that night." Hayely rested her hand briefly on his arm. "You should let me be the one who decides what I'm willing to give."

Gary looked at her with no little surprise on his face. "Alright then. We would have to spend a lot of time together to make it convincing. We'd have to get photos taken together. We'd have to be seen around town and leak the news of our nuptials. And in five or so more months, we'd have to face the music when the gossip about our divorce spreads like wildfire. Does that sound like any fun to you?"

Hayely returned Gary's gaze thoughtfully and began to fold the blanket. She already told him she planned to resign from her job and would have to move out after the arrangement was over anyway. If she moved out of state, which she'd considered, she wouldn't have to deal with any of the fallout — not the way he would.

"I think I could consider doing all those things. But, what happens when your Mr. Bellmark comes to visit and I haven't a clue as to why he's visiting?"

Gary tapped his fingertip against his bottom lip. Telling her about his promise would take one of the greatest leaps of faith he'd ever made. There wasn't another soul who knew of his past other than Charlie and the Bellmarks. As a man who had used words sparingly up until now, he wasn't even sure he was capable of letting such critical ones flow.

"You're right," he acknowledged slowly. "But I have to believe you'll take what I say to the grave. I'm — very private."

She made the sign of a cross over her

heart with her finger. "Your secret is my secret."

Gary drew in a breath and continued in a voice that sounded more like a rumble. "I met Charlie about twenty years ago at a small, privately run orphanage in Maine. We grew up together there."

"What happened to your parents?"

"I was told they'd drowned in a boating accident, but I never knew for sure. I just remember getting tossed from place to place until I landed there with Mr. and Mrs. Bellmark. They were absolutely incredible. Those two treated all of us — all forty-five of us — as if we were their own natural children. They never even forgot a birthday."

"I wish you'd told me some of this earlier. You've come a long way, Gary Tarleton. I can't imagine most people achieving what you have."

"They just haven't been given the proper chance, which is where my promise comes in. When I was about ten, I got dressed up in my best Sunday clothes and marched into Mr. Bellmark's office. I told him that I was never going to let his home for boys end up like the others. I promised that I'd do whatever it took to make sure the orphans who lived there always had it the best, always learned what a family was the way he and his wife had taught us."

"So where do I figure into all of this?"

"Mr. Bellmark made a promise to me, too. He said he would see the place bulldozed when he died rather than let some typical state-trained social worker touch a hand to it. He told me that if I grew up honorably, made a strong marriage, and could pass the right values on to the children, then he'd consider letting me try to live up to my promise."

Hayely thought for a moment. "But isn't it dishonest tricking him into thinking something about you that isn't true?"

Gary's gaze felt steadily more intense. "But, I have the value system, Hayely. And someday I'll have the family I want for real. It just hasn't happened for me yet." He hung his head for a moment and ran his hand over his chin. "And I know a very kind, stable, religious local couple there who can't have children of their own. They would love nothing more than to move in and run the place. They remind me so much of Mr. and Mrs. Bellmark that it's scary. I have the money to put those kids through school, all the way to their doctorates if they want. Mr. Bellmark used to take us all every Sunday to this old church down the road. I can pay to keep a pastor there and repair the building when it's necessary. I —"

"Ok already. You've won me over." Hayely was afraid she'd have to put her hand over his mouth to cut him off. She laughed brightly.

Gary stood quickly and Hayely rose to stand beside him. He'd said more in the last five minutes with Hayely than he had to all the women in his past combined. And it felt wonderful.

She judged his mood with a glance. "I'm glad you feel better." She looked up at him, her shining eyes explaining silently that his elation was contagious. She was genuinely happy simply because he was.

Gary caught his breath as he looked at her for much longer than ever intended. He bent and placed a chaste kiss on her forehead, wanting to linger and not quite daring.

"Must be a friendly office you've got." Hayely blushed in spite of her efforts to sound collected.

"I got carried away." He quickly walked toward the door. "You're easy to get carried away with, Mrs. Tarleton."

"Knock off the 'Mrs. Tarleton' bit, will you?" she teased. "You know, I think a real wife would be your undoing. And that would be a good thing."

Gary closed her door tightly behind him as he left her room and then forced his feet to move forward until the urge to kiss her had passed.

Charlie grinned as he lounged lazily on the back porch swing. The photographer had positioned Gary and Hayely in front of a fountain for the next round of pictures. He'd lost count of how many rolls of film she'd already gone through.

"No, it doesn't look right from here. I think they should sit closer. Hold hands maybe." Charlie pretended not to catch the sinister glare Gary gave him when the lady with the fancy camera wasn't looking. He chuckled to himself when she suggested the couple do exactly as Charlie had suggested.

"And wouldn't it be great," he called out, "to get one of them kissing. It would be so romantic."

But from watching Gary and Hayely, no one would suspect they weren't looking at a real husband and wife. They certainly had their act down to a fine scientific study of romance. Each time Gary looked down into Hayely's eyes, the two seemed to get stuck there until the photographer laughed and bent them into a new pose.

And then there was the unique fact that

Hayely's bare knee seemed to draw Gary's rough hand to it like a magnet of sorts. Sometimes Hayely would place her own hand over his and fidget with his wedding band while it rested on her leg. Did either of them notice what they were doing? Charlie wondered.

"And that does it," the photographer finished. "I can have these developed by the end of the week if that works for you."

"Fine. Thank you," Gary said in typically gruff fashion, then nodded for Charlie to see the woman to her car. Hayely gave Gary an exasperated look as if he'd been horrible somehow. "What? Don't know her, don't care to chat with her any more than I need to."

"You could at least put a full sentence together for the woman. She did come here on really, really short notice after all. Not to mention on her day off."

Gary shot Hayely a sidelong glance. "Going to keep me civilized are you, Mrs. Tarleton?"

"Mr. Tarleton, I don't think it's possible." Hayely laughed out loud, the sound of it mixing with the bubbling water in the fountain behind them. "Besides, I thought you were going to quit calling me that."

When she awoke that morning, she'd

wondered if things might be tense between her and Gary. She worried if he was the type to feel embarrassment at the slightest revealed feeling. He might treat her like a leper because she'd been the one to witness the inner workings of Gary Tarleton, unsociable tycoon extraordinaire.

But as always, all it took was one rolling word from his soothing voice and the touch of his hand brushing her elbow, and she felt completely at home in the world. It was odd how someone so seemingly reticent had that effect on people, on her.

Gary placed his hand protectively on Hayely's shoulder as she walked up the porch steps. She'd lost track of how many times he'd come close to walking back into her room that night. To apologize? To see if she would have let him kiss her? She didn't know. His hand had been on that doorknob a hundred times, but he'd turned around and walked away just one time more than that.

The possibility of creating a stable family for real had just never seemed in the cards for him, had it? She guessed there'd been too many women with ulterior motives, no one who could draw him away from the office.

Hayely looked skeptically up at Gary.

He'd fallen into one of his long silences on the way into the house, and she was too scared of his answer to offer a penny for his thoughts.

"Where should we go today?" he asked.

"Go?" she asked as he turned and headed for the front of the house instead.

"No time like the present for getting those rumors flying. If we start today, we'll have a good bit of gossip coverage before the Chamber of Commerce banquet on Wednesday night."

"What banquet is that?" She ran to catch him.

"I've had a dozen different invitations from women to the banquet already and here I am, married to the only one who has never even heard of it."

"Life's funny, ain't it?" she asked.

"The banquet is the biggest event this spring. Maybe all year even. The annual awards ceremony is always held at it, and just about every major business in the state sends someone to attend."

"Is it very formal?" Hayely had left her evening gowns in a box somewhere in the back of her parents' garage. She'd never imagined she might have a use for them anytime soon.

"Fairly." He was glad he'd parked in the

driveway last time instead of pulling into the garage.

"Gary, I don't have anything to wear. I don't want people to see you with me looking like I've dressed out of a thrift store." She felt tears threaten to sting her eyes. Why on earth had she let Kathy's cruel words bother her so? Days later, they still hurt.

Gary was thoroughly taken aback by her reaction. "Hey. What's that look for? Seems to me we've just found our excuse to go out on the town. I think a few boutiques are probably open on Sunday."

Hayely wiped her eyes with the back of her hands. "I'd love to go shopping. Can I get shoes, too?"

Gary laughed outright. "I'm sure you have fifty pairs in your closet and none of them will do." He held open the door to his big truck for her and watched as she climbed high up inside.

"You have a truck," she stated flatly as he shut the driver's side door.

"Yes."

"Why?" she asked.

"Why? It's a long walk to work."

She smiled in spite of herself. "I mean most people with a house like yours would be trying to prove something. I imagined a garage littered with Ferraris and Porsches."

"I never understood those pretentious types either. You know, the types who run out and buy useless, expensive watches."

His sense of humor charmed her. "My father probably has a fraction of the money you do and he drives a Rolls Royce. But he wouldn't spend that much money on a watch I don't think."

"If he's that well off, why couldn't you have just called him and asked for a loan when you stepped on my watch?" He shrugged and adjusted the rearview mirror.

"My father is convinced I need to do one specific thing and be with one specific kind of man. I can't stand the men he approves of and the thing he wants me to do bores me to tears, and vice versa. I'd rather be poor and happy than — don't even make me start thinking about it — indebted."

"Why not be rich and happy?" Gary shoved the truck into gear and rolled out of the driveway.

"Life's not always a fairy tale, you know."

"Well," he said, "for today we'll both be rich and happy then. We'll find a stunning gown for you, drink caramel lattes until we're sick, and come home to a good night's sleep in a warm house. Can't do much better than that."

"You make life sound like one big carnival." Hayely rolled her eyes and sighed deeply. "Too bad I have to go into the office tomorrow."

Gary stopped talking as he caught a glimpse of himself in the mirror. He'd been out on too many sites lately. He wasn't even presentable in his current state and he'd just had pictures taken. At least Hayely looked good. The new distress in her voice bothered him and his gaze shifted back to her.

"Still think you'll get fired when they find out you're married?" He sounded unconcerned, but he wasn't. He felt he needed to watch Kathy Mark closely for some reason, and he never ignored his instincts.

Hayely nodded. "They're just looking for something to call my trustworthiness into question. They'll say I was deceptive or something along those lines. Let's not talk about it anymore. It's not your problem to deal with. I'm handling it."

Gary grasped the steering wheel tighter. A couple weeks or so ago, he'd hired one of Kathy Mark's former employees, and the grateful man had painted him a vivid picture of the woman a few days later. In fact, it had taken his new employee days to stop flinching like a beaten dog every time a supervisor so much as spoke to him. The thought of someone treating Hayely the way he suspected she was being treated made Gary clench his teeth. Darn if Kathy Mark was going to get a shred of business tossed her way after that.

"I've heard about that Mark woman," he said at last. "Just let me know if she gives you too much trouble. And by the way, that watch was going to be a birthday gift for Charlie."

"Knowing you now, that makes sense." She noticed that the only piece of jewelry on him was his wedding band. He didn't wear a watch very often either.

The truck's big engine pulled them effortlessly down the freeway and off an exit to a line of expensive clothing stores not far from downtown.

Gary jumped out of the truck, his heavy boots hitting the pavement in a well-practiced motion as he strode around to open Hayely's door. He paused for a moment with his hands resting lightly on her waist and looked up at her tense face.

"You'd be the prettiest woman at the party even if you showed up in your paint-splattered sweatpants," he said loudly.

Hayely placed her hands on his shoulders and let him swing her down from the truck. "Charlie said you were charming when you wanted to be. Anyone watching would think we're really an item. You're good, boss." She winked mysteriously at him.

That familiar and much-too-serious expression crossed Gary's face. For a moment he looked extremely solemn. Was she genuinely flirting with him? Usually when women spoke to him with that tone, it was just before they asked for something. Years of conditioning threatened to kick in. Of course she wasn't flirting. Hayely knew where the line was and she hadn't seemed tempted to cross it.

Hayely studied the panic on his face. "I think I like your usual grouchy, antisocial self better." She turned on her heel and walked off ahead of him toward the first boutique. "Come on," she called with a laugh.

Gary breathed a sigh of relief and caught up to her with only a few long strides. Was she as nervous as he suddenly was? He wasn't sure if he could make the charade believable in front of an audience. He caught her hand up firmly in his grasp and held on to it with far more strength than was necessary.

"What happened to the charm?" she whispered.

"You're my wife," he growled. "Should I

ask permission to hold your hand in public?" Despite his tone, there was the sound of a smile in his words.

"There now. That's the fictitious husband I know." Hayely gave Gary's hand a quick squeeze and walked into the shop with him in tow.

As a little bell on top of the door rang, the salesclerk immediately recognized Gary and rushed toward the door. Her short black hair was so dark that it might look almost blue in the right lighting. Spiked with a hard styling gel, it shook with the impact of her heels on the floor as she nearly tripped over herself to reach Gary first.

"Mr. Tarleton, welcome. What can we help you find today?"

"Evening gowns," came his clipped answer.

"Evening gowns we've got," the clerk said as she clasped her red-tipped fingers together and visibly fought to calm her nerves. "We had a whole new line come in just this morning. Is the dress for your . . . sister?" She looked meaningfully toward Hayely and waited.

Gary smiled stiffly at Hayely, his teeth held a bit too tightly together. "Would you mind handling this alone, honey? I'm out of my element amongst women's clothing, and

I need to pick up a few things."

Hayely frowned. Would he leave this woman with the impression that he was her brother? What was she supposed to say to her if he did?

"I can do it," was all she responded.

"Good." He leaned down and planted a sweet kiss directly on her mouth. Then he turned toward the awestruck clerk as he placed his credit card into Hayely's hand. "We're a really close family."

Hayely suppressed a shocked smile as Gary walked back out the door. Her hand flew to the place his lips had just touched. Already she could hear the other clerks whispering frantically from behind the counter. At first they thought Hayely was a girlfriend, but one of them had spotted the matching platinum wedding bands.

"Can you help me find a dress?" she finally asked.

The clerk came to her senses as Hayely held up the plastic card with a credit limit she could only imagine in her hand. "I think we can find something suitable. Is it for the Chamber banquet?"

Hayely nodded and said quietly, "I've never been to one before. I really could use your advice on what to wear."

The clerk took a look at Hayely and

desperately wanted to dislike her. After all, she'd come in on the arm of the man she and her friends had fantasized about for years. But in spite of herself, one look at Hayely's sincerely warm expression and a new train of thought crossed her mind.

"Mrs. Tarleton, I presume? By the time we get through with you, every snobbish, highbrow socialite is going to turn green with envy. Just you watch."

"Thank you," Hayely whispered. "You have no idea how much I appreciate it."

The clerk held out her hand, "I'm Carla."

Hayely shook her hand. "Hayely."

"First things first. You're going to be surrounded by a lot of bleached blonde testaments to plastic surgery. They'll all be wearing black, red, or if this year is anything like last year — pink. The sequins and spaghetti straps will all start to look the same. You'll want something different. Something classy."

"Sounds fine with me. I don't go well with glitz."

Carla escorted Hayely into an enormous, posh dressing room. "You wait right here and I'll bring the dresses to you. I've already got a few ideas."

Hayely unbuttoned her clothes and took the first gown over the curtain from Carla.

There was lavender followed by something scarlet. Black, silver, and green all fell by the wayside. Velvet, satin, and a filmy material like gauze were all cast aside in no time. Some of the outfits were too revealing, others not revealing enough, and still more hung all wrong around her curves.

"We don't have time to specially design something for you by Wednesday night, but we can alter anything you'd like," Carla offered hopefully.

Dress after dress, Hayely tried them all on until at last she and Carla found the perfect design. Just as the decision was made, the bell over the door told them Gary had returned to reclaim his wife.

"Hayely Tarleton, just you wait until your husband sees this dress — sees you and that cute little figure of yours shown off in this dress," Carla whispered with a contagious excitement. "He won't even notice the rest of the party."

"You have to promise not to show it to him. I want it to be a surprise." She couldn't wait to see the look on Gary's face when he saw the dress she'd chosen. She only hoped it would live up to his expectations — that she would.

Carla splayed her long fingers out over her heart. "Oh, it's so romantic. I wish I had a nice man to be romantic for." On impulse she gave Hayely a quick hug. "You're going to do great. And if you ever need anything else, don't hesitate to ask for me. Good luck."

Hayely thanked her and signed the credit card slip while trying not to look too closely at the obscene total printed on it. Good luck? She had the feeling she was going to need it.

Chapter Five

Monday morning started with its usual amount of chaos. For the first time, Hayely left her wedding band securely on her finger. She'd been careful to take it off and hide it in the zipper compartment of her purse before work each day. But she knew she had to tell the human resources department about her marriage, and just seeing the ring on her finger brought Gary's confident voice of reassurance to mind. They'd laughed all the way home from the boutique the day before just from imagining the reaction their news was sure to get.

Hayely locked the big front doors of the house and tugged on them for good measure. She'd hurried getting ready for work that morning, but found she had missed Gary by an hour or two. He always left so early. She wanted to get to the office as soon as possible anyway. As self-defense, she'd begun sending Kathy a good morning greeting via e-mail so that the time of day marked plainly on the printout would show she'd come in early. Hayely could only imagine what Kathy's new tactics would be once she caught on to Hayely's job-preservation strategy.

As she stepped down into the circular driveway, she froze. She scanned the curb up and down, but her old rattletrap car was nowhere to be seen. Had someone stolen it? Mistaken it for junk and towed it? Her mind reeled. The only vehicle left in the place was a shiny new BMW parked where her poor car used to be. She wondered where the car could have come from — it didn't look like something Gary would drive. He would barely fit inside it!

A bit of white paper flapping from under the windshield wiper caught her attention and she walked hesitantly toward the car. Its silver paint sparkled in the morning sunlight. She could imagine someone driving in it high along winding ocean cliffs with the water churning far below. If she had a car like this, she'd put the top down and tie a long silk scarf around her neck just to feel it blow along softly around her.

She sighed, pulled out the note and read it aloud. "Hayely," it began in Gary's hand-writing, "I want you to have this car. Call it a job perk. The keys are in the ignition."

Hayely folded up the note calmly and stuffed it into her purse. Then she pulled open the car door with a giggle and jumped inside. The smell of new leather surrounded her as she ran her hand over the seats. New red leather. "Wow," she said to herself, "the seats are even heated."

And then another thought struck her. He'd gotten rid of her real car. The irritation from that notion sent tiny stabs through her insides. She'd scraped together the five-hundred-dollar down payment to buy that car on her own, and then eked out the remaining five hundred dollars in monthly payments all on her own, too. It was the first thing she'd ever completely earned by herself. And Gary Tarleton hadn't even bothered to consult with her about it before giving it away.

As she turned the key in the car's ignition, she couldn't help but sigh again. It truly was a gorgeous car — exactly what she'd drive if she were really the wife of a wealthy businessman. Maybe she would drive it for a day or two until Gary could get her real car back for her. After all, when people saw her in a car like this, there would be no doubt she'd really married the renowned Gary Tarleton. Maybe that's what he'd been thinking all along.

As usual, Hayely was nearly the first person to arrive in the office. She would have arrived earlier if she'd been able to find all the gears in her new car a little better. Someone had already put a pot of coffee on to brew, but the lights in her area were off. No sooner than she'd turned on her computer, sent out the routine e-mail and sorted through the faxes, the rest of the staff began pouring in.

Her hands were almost clammy as she watched the human resources staff settle into their chairs. She drew in a deep breath and walked into the manager's office.

"Do you have a minute?" Hayely asked. "I just need to make some changes to my paperwork."

"Sure. What kind of changes?"

There was no backing out now. "I got married," she answered, running the three words together as if they were one syllable.

The human resources manager got up from her desk and walked over the Hayely. "Congratulations," she squealed. "I had no idea you were even engaged. What's his name? What does he do?"

"Well —"

The sound of Kathy Mark's demanding voice rang from the doorway behind her.

"There you both are. I don't like to see empty chairs. You know Dee, don't you? She's just made senior vice president and isn't it wonderful, she's here from Arkansas this week."

Hayely smiled at Kathy's stout, square-faced daughter. It was common knowledge that Dee Mark's brief stints as a bartender and used car saleswoman had hardly prepared her for an executive position. It grated on Hayely's nerves whenever she was asked to prepare documents that Dee should have been doing herself. With her meager month of experience, Hayely thought it was like the blind leading the blind — except one of the blind was making about six figures a year more than the other for the same expertise. No wonder the company scrambled for work.

Dee gave a hearty laugh and thumped Hayely on the back. "Good to finally see you in person."

"Nice to meet you, too," Hayely replied. Was that beer she smelled in the air?

The human resources manager spoke up. "Kathy, Hayely was just telling me she's gotten married."

Kathy's eyebrows rose. "Oh?"

The manager asked, "What's your new last name?"

"I haven't decided to change it yet. I might keep my maiden name for a while."

Dee hooted again. "That's what I did, too. Mercy, we Mark women don't stay married long enough for it to be worth a name change anyway!" Her ruddy face turned even redder as she laughed at her own joke. "What's his name?"

"Gary," Hayely answered softly. She had definitely picked up the scent of alcohol again. She'd seen Dee's brother, Darryl, in the office from time to time and thought she'd caught of whiff of booze on his breath, too. It was sad really, and in spite of herself, Hayely felt her dislike turn to pity.

Kathy looked coolly down her nose at Hayely. "Speaking of men named Gary, I hear Gary Tarleton is going to the Chamber Banquet this Wednesday evening. I'd like you to see if you can find a good hairdresser for Dee."

Dee pointed to her short sandy blonde hair. "Can't go looking this way in front of Gary."

"You know Gary — Mr. Tarleton well?" Hayely asked.

Kathy interrupted the start of her daughter's answer. "Of course we do. We've been friends for ages. From the impression I got, he'd like to spend some time with Dee this year."

"I see." Hayely fought to keep a laugh from building inside her. If she knew anything, it was what Gary would think of the entire Mark family. With his sense of family values and business protocol, he wouldn't so much as look in their direction.

Kathy squinted at Hayely's clothing again and gave a tight little smile. "To tell you the truth, I wouldn't have thought you'd have heard of Gary Tarleton or the Chamber Banquet for that matter. I'm surprised."

"I only recently heard of both." Hayely smoothed her dark grey skirt and checked very, very subtly to see if her yellow silk shirt was still tucked in correctly.

"Well then I'm sure you've heard how prestigious it is for a firm to be invited to attend the event."

Hayely bit into her lower lip and looked demurely down at the floor to keep from laughing. Gary had already told her that every business in the state was allowed to attend virtually at will. All they had to do was pay a membership fee.

She breathed and said, "Does Dee have a dress? I know of a very nice, exclusive boutique downtown. I can write down the directions if you'd like."

Dee pounded Hayely on the back again. "That would be great. I'd love to find something that would really stand out — maybe a little strapless number with red sequins. Or how about pink? I know Gary's mad for that color on the ladies."

Hayely went back to her desk, cheerfully scribbled out an address, and drew a quick map for Dee. If nothing else, her helpfulness would keep Kathy and her truck-driveresque daughter out of the office and away from her. She wouldn't hear any threats about being fired that day. She smiled broadly as she watched the loathsome pair walk out the door.

The day flew by joyfully and before she knew it, she was virtually sailing down the freeway in her new sports car. Too bad she'd have to give it up in just a few more months. It felt as if the machine were designed for her and her alone.

Hayely sprinted into the house, kicked off her shoes in the marble foyer, and ran upstairs to change clothes. The deliverymen had been at it again. During the day, the formerly empty weight room had been filled with top-notch training equipment and heavy sets of free weights. She'd taken the liberty of ordering a treadmill and exercise bike, too. Thank goodness the delivery company had set up and installed every-thing. Most of it looked too heavy for her to even budge.

And the living room furniture had arrived! Hayely was almost giddy. The electricians had obviously been by to wire in the new overhead lighting, which glowed with an understated cordiality. With the intricate carvings Gary had designed into the door frames and windowsills, it was easy to add depth and elegance to the room.

She had chosen comfortable, richly uphol-stered chairs and a cream-colored sofa with a sophisticated brocade pattern that stood out just a shade darker against its back-ground. The ornate fireplace screen, coffee table, and end tables hadn't arrived yet. And more leafy green houseplants were desper-ately needed. But day-by-day, the empty house was transforming from an unloved address to a comfortable home.

Dressed in baggy sweatpants with her hair up in a messy ponytail, Hayely surveyed the rooms around her. She was far ahead of schedule, so far that she just might take a break from decorating. She'd picked up another new cookbook at the library on the way home and couldn't wait to try out the key lime cheesecake recipe in it.

She hummed along to the tune of the

mixer as she whipped up first one cheesecake and then the next. Maybe she was going overboard, but there were three variations she just had to try while she had the time. Besides, she'd taken the easy route with dinner and just made a pot roast with potatoes and carrots for Charlie and Gary. She'd sampled them all until she was stuffed.

With a smile, she brushed some flour from her hands onto her baggy pants and stood back to admire her work. Key lime, raspberry swirl, and chocolate chip cheesecakes lined the counter. Right on cue, she heard Charlie walk into the kitchen first, followed closely behind by Gary. Were they coming home earlier in the evenings now? It seemed so.

She dropped her dishrag onto the counter and looked up. "Dinner's on the table, guys. Enjoy. I've been admiring the pool for the last six weeks and I think I'm finally going to try it out."

She grinned and walked past them as casually as possible. Could Gary tell how rattled she got when he walked into the room after a day at some construction site or another? Was it obvious that the dust in his hair and his sun-bronzed skin made it hard not to simply stand and stare at him?

He was easy on the eyes, she'd give him that.

"Who was that woman?" Charlie asked with a laugh.

Gary shook his head and grabbed a plate. "My guess is a woman whose boss was out of the office all day. I saw the witch driving downtown today."

"That bad, huh?"

Gary nodded between bites. "She can cook. You know, I'd tell her to quit her job and just let me take care of her expenses if I didn't think she'd be offended."

Charlie bit into a juicy, butter-soaked carrot and moaned as if in heaven. "I've been looking over the accounting records for all this decorating she's been doing."

"How much has this set me back so far?"

"She hasn't come close to spending even half of what we thought it'd take. And you know what? She hasn't bought a thing for herself. Make-up, shampoo, books — her cell phone bill. Chewing gum, for Pete's sake. She's been paying for all those things with her own cash. I saw some of the store receipts sitting in the garbage can the other day."

Gary paused with a chunk of onion on his fork. "You're kidding?"

Charlie shook his head. "Nope."

"I understand independence, but she's contributing way more than her share to the plan. She's earned a little fair treatment."

"Given all that zest for independence, I wonder what she thought of the expensive car," Charlie mused and shot a meaningful look at Gary.

Gary tossed down his napkin. He hadn't considered that she might have a lukewarm or even negative reaction to his generosity. That she hadn't mentioned the car at all couldn't be good.

Gary walked in his sock feet all the way across the house, through a newly magnificent exercise room, and directly to the indoor pool. When had she found the time to pick out weight lifting equipment? He smiled. After lifting lumber all day, he couldn't imagine what use he'd ever have for a bench press. Maybe for all those other days when he wound up stuck behind a desk.

The telltale scent of chlorine wafted toward him as he opened and closed the door to the pool. Hayely turned around to face him as she treaded in water up to her neck. The cobalt tiles under her feet emphasized the water's blue reflection along the walls.

"I haven't been swimming in ages," she said. "I'd forgotten how good it could feel. This is like having access to a private company spa or something."

Gary looked down through the water. The pool was too sparsely lighted and the water rippled just enough to obscure his view of what looked to be a simple black swimsuit.

"I wanted to talk to you about the car."

Hayely swam to the edge of the pool and lifted herself out onto the cement edge to sit on her towel. "I wanted to talk to you about that, too." She squeezed some water out of her moisture-darkened hair and wrapped herself in another large towel.

He forced himself to meet her eyes and think of the reason he'd sought her out. "Did you drive it today?"

"I did. And I understand you probably got it so that I'd look more the part, but I have to admit I'm a little angry that you junked my car. I worked hard for it." She sputtered as she dabbed the water off her face. "Personal property."

Her words caught him by surprise. "Appearances were definitely a benefit. But mainly, I was afraid the heap you were driving would break down on the road somewhere. It wasn't reliable and I thought you'd like the style of the new one."

"But you should have at least talked to me first, Gary. My car might not have been much, but it was still my car. You know, I could press grand theft auto charges I think. And what do you suggest I do at the end of our contract when I don't have any transportation?"

He hated that she bristled every time he offered her something harmless. No one should have grown accustomed to fighting at every turn just to be heard. Now she was looking at him with such an expression of hurt stubbornness that his heart turned over in his chest.

"Hayely," he whispered. "Your car is sitting in the garage. I asked Charlie to put it there for you. I'm not accustomed to stealing my employees' property. I just wanted you to be safe on the way to work."

Hayely dropped her defiant gaze. "Thank you, I guess."

"Sometimes I think you mistake acts of kindness for disrespect."

"I mistake them for charity." She smiled weakly. "I'm still getting used to this being independent thing. And this contract of ours. But I'm trying not to get too comfortable in this house of yours."

Comfortable? That was the last word Gary would use to describe how he felt sitting next to his scantily clad "wife." "Do you at least like the car a little?"

His gruff voice sounded so eager to please that Hayely reached out and took his hand in hers. "I do like it," she said as she looked into his hazel eyes. "It's perfect for me."

"So you'll try to get used to it?"

She nodded.

"You know what I'm trying to get used to?" he asked in a murmur. "The way you cook dinner for me and Charlie when you definitely don't have to. Each and every piece of furniture picked out with me in mind. Coming home to a real home. I appreciate your work more than you know. I'd never expected so much."

Hayely's eyes swam like mercury as she looked up at his handsome face. "For a man of few words, you seem to know all the right ones."

"Yeah," he growled. "I don't know what's wrong with me."

"Must be the chlorine fumes."

With a breath of resignation and a smile he pulled farther away from her. "Back to business. Have you heard anything yet?"

"No. But the rumor mill should be grinding out gossip in grand style by tomorrow, I have a feeling."

"Did they say anything at work when you

told them you'd gotten hitched?"

Hayely shook her head. "Not really. They seemed to have other things on their minds."

"Why don't you just resign from that place?"

"And do what?" she asked.

"Interior design work for me — full-time until you find another job. You've done so much for me, why can't you let me do something for you?"

"Thanks, boss. But I have to pass. I want to find something I'm good at and do it well. I can't have someone always walking ahead of me to smooth out all the bumps in the road." She paused in thought. "Besides, I have to leave here in just a few months. Best not to get too attached — to this place."

"Forget about the interior design or any kind of job at my company then. Find some new adventure. You'd at least have a roof over your head. You're welcome to stay as long as you'd like after Mr. Bellmark sells me the boys' home."

"As what? An ex-fake-wife? A houseguest? People would really start to talk then."

"Let them. It was just an idea." Gary turned away as she jumped back into the pool and the moment was broken. He stood to return to his cold dinner. "Something to think on."

Hayely's mind was far from her work the next morning. Sure, she'd arrived there early, but had done nothing but stare blankly at her computer monitor ever since. What was wrong with her anyway? Her conversation with Gary the night before, that's what.

She was a valued asset and employee; he'd made that much clear beside the pool the night before. He'd said exactly what he should have said, so everything should have been well and good. And yet the monitor continued to hold her unseeing attention.

A sudden cacophony of screeching female voices jarred her from her stupor and she sat up straight in her chair. She recognized Kathy's and Dee's voices immediately, but it took a moment to pinpoint the chief financial officer's and the human resource manager's in the mix. She thought there might be a couple others standing there, too.

Dee's voice was nothing better than a controlled bellow most of the time. ". . . and then one of the clerks told me that he's bringing a date or something to the banquet with him. Can you believe it?"

The CFO chimed in. "Did they say who she was?"

"No," Dee said petulantly. "They said the clerk who had helped her knew more, but it was her day off and she hadn't told them anything."

"Typical incompetence," Kathy added. "None of them even recognized her."

"That's right. They'd never seen her before. They said she was really beautiful, though."

"He can't be serious about her," Kathy reasoned. "If he were actually dating some out-of-state floozy again, it would have been in the papers by now. Everyone would have already seen her picture."

"Maybe she's a relative?" one of the other voices suggested.

Dee's voice took on a conspiratorial tone. "One of them even swore she saw a wedding ring."

"On whose finger?"

"Gary's?"

"The mystery woman's?"

"Whose?"

Hayely smiled into her hand. The whispers were flying so fast and furious that she could scarcely keep up with them all. She took a sip of coffee and hoped the pack would stay just out of sight. She didn't know if she could resist baiting them if they walked around the corner and included her in the conversation.

"I didn't think to ask," Dee answered as a hush fell.

Kathy rounded the corner and stood in front of Hayely's desk. "Did you arrange a hairstyling appointment for Dee?"

Hayely handed her a card with all the information on it. "She can get in about two hours before the banquet begins."

Kathy swiped the card away. "Fine. I have another assignment for you." She tossed a résumé and a series of yellow sticky notes onto Hayely's desk. "I want you to send a letter to this man at this address." She pointed to one of the notes. "You'll have to figure out my handwriting because I don't have time to explain it to you. Tell him we can provide the qualifications he needs for his projects. I want you to add the credentials on this piece of paper here to this résumé and include it with the letter."

Hayely stared at the employee's résumé for a moment and read through the notes. "I think there may be some kind of mistake here. This employee doesn't have that degree or any of those certifications —"

Kathy put her hands on her hips for emphasis. Her voice was rising to the verge of a yell. "Have you looked at my business card lately? It says 'president' and that means I can do any damn thing I want. Maybe if you ever run your own company someday, which I doubt, you'll understand."

"I might be able to find a different résumé —" Hayely had a fleeting urge to stand up and tell the woman what she thought of her, but something inside her shrunk. She knew that half the people in the office were listening to Kathy's treatment of her just then. How could they not overhear every humiliating word?

Kathy cut her off again. "Don't get argumentative with me, sweetie. I'll do whatever it takes to get that contract." With that, she walked off in a huff down the hall.

As was always the case after one of Kathy's tirades, all the staff looked down with red faces at their desks, afraid to look up at each other. Hayely had seen her boss abuse people a hundred times over, but never had it been directed so hostilely toward her. Hayely walked in a daze to the break room to wash out her coffee cup. What should she do? Try to talk to Kathy? Go home for the day? She had no idea.

With a fresh cup of coffee in her shaking hand, she started back around the maze of hallways to her desk. Just as she approached the human resources department, Kathy's voice reached her through a crack in the door to the manager's office.

"Place an ad online," Kathy hissed. "Let's start interviewing people as soon as possible. I just can't tolerate that kind of disobedience. We'll get someone lined up for her job before we let her go. No downtime."

"Don't you think we should give her some kind of reprimand or training?" the other woman suggested.

"No. I want the unprofessional little goodie goodie out of here. If I can't trust her to simply follow my instructions without questioning them, then there's no point in having her here."

Hayely's hand flew to her mouth. She was actually going to be fired for having a sense of ethics? Hayely ran back to her desk and did the first thing she could think of — grab her purse and leave.

She passed the cowering receptionist who looked up at her with understanding. "If Kathy asks where I am, tell her I got suddenly sick to my stomach and went home for the day."

Hayely was in tears by the time she walked through the front door to Gary's house. She sat down at the kitchen table with the remaining half of the raspberry cheesecake and a spoon. It looked like Gary and Charlie had eaten the other cakes the night before.

She pulled the tissue box closer to her as her sobs came one after the other. She'd messed up everything. No one wanted her, and with the way Kathy Mark tried to blacklist ex-employees, she'd never find a decent job in this city if she tried. She knew Kathy would fire her within the next couple of weeks. Gary would hire her — he'd already offered. But she didn't want to work for him. She couldn't quite understand why, but being treated like hired help by Gary Tarleton after the six months were up sounded like nothing short of torture. The thought of her situation with Gary brought on a whole new wave of tears.

Out on the highway, Gary pushed the accelerator down hard with his heavy work boots. The truck's big engine roared toward the house as he shifted into overdrive. He almost never heard from his gardener during the day, but the man had called to tell him he'd seen Hayely walk into the house crying. Had she been in an accident? Had something happened to a family member? When the gardener didn't have any answers, a hundred more terrifying options raced through Gary's mind.

He turned the truck sharply into the driveway and hit the brakes with a loud squeal. He banged the thick door shut behind him as he lumbered for the house. As he crossed the foyer, he heard the unmistakable sound of a woman's sniffling.

Hayely wiped her eyes quickly and forced a smile as Gary burst into the room. With his shirt half untucked and his eyes wide, he paused and stood awkwardly.

"Are you alright?" he breathed out as he walked over to her.

Hayely nodded vigorously and dabbed at her nose. "I just had a really bad morning. I'll be fine."

"No one's hurt then?"

"No. Just my pride."

Gary exhaled harshly in relief as he sat down beside her. Should he put his arm around her? He had absolutely no experience dealing with upset females, and this one had progressed all the way to crying.

"Tell me what happened."

The rich, full resonance of his voice instantly began to work its magic on her and the tears slowed. Slowly, haltingly, Hayely began to describe everything that had happened to her that morning and everything she'd witnessed over the past weeks.

"I've never worked in another office," she concluded. "Is it supposed to be like that?"

A muscle near Gary's jaw clenched and unclenched. So help him, if he saw the witch again he'd strangle her with his bare hands. How dare someone like that Mark woman make someone as wonderful as Hayely cry? The woman was trash in an expensive suit and Hayely was so thoroughly kind — so kind she didn't know how to stand up for herself at the right times.

"No," he soothed. "It's never supposed to be like that. No one is entitled to treat another person that way, company president or otherwise." He scooted his chair closer to Hayely's and put his arms around her at last. "And from what you described, it sounds very much like she's defrauding her clients."

"It's not just clients," she sniffed. "I've seen her print out one job description and salary range, and after someone accepts that job on those terms, she changes everything on them the week after."

Gary shook his head. "Trust me when I tell you this will come back to haunt her. When word gets out around the industry — and it will — you'll see the best example of instant karma imaginable. You don't need to be ruthless to be successful."

He bent down without thinking, stopping himself just before he was about to kiss the top of her head on impulse. He accidentally breathed in the delicate scent of her flowery shampoo and hoped she was too upset to notice what he'd almost done.

"What do you want to do, Hayely?" he asked when she fell into silence.

"I don't know, but it definitely isn't shuffling paperwork. I went to school for a degree in biology. Did I ever tell you that? My father wanted me to go on to medical school. I hated biology. Pre-med would have been even worse."

"You have to find your passion and then build a career from it."

Hayely blew her nose unceremoniously. "How did you make your money, Gary? I have no idea how you did all this."

"When I came to live with Mr. and Mrs. Bellmark, they arranged for me to make a dollar a week sweeping floors. I saved it up like a grade school miser. No candy for me that year. When I had fifty dollars, I asked Mr. Bellmark what I should do with it and he told me about something called the stock market."

"You invested in Wall Street at age ten?"

"Yup. And I quadrupled my money. So I cashed out the original investment and reinvested the rest. When I'd made enough money, I cashed some more out and bought a car."

"A car? You couldn't even drive it at that age."

"It was a mess. I bought it cheap and spent my evenings learning how to repair it. I conned a local mechanic into letting me borrow some tools. When I had it looking the way I wanted, I sold it."

"Sounds like you had business in your blood from the start."

"Well, I turned fifty dollars into several thousand dollars within another year, if that's what you mean. To make a long story short, I kept buying and selling. Started with small pieces of land, then houses, and so on. And of course, I kept up with the stock market investing, too."

"So how did you wind up starting your own business?" she asked.

"After fixing up all those houses, I figured I could do a better job building them from the ground up. I don't know how Mr. Bellmark did it, but he got me into college early. Scholarships. Loans. But I got my degree in architecture and went on to a master's in business administration. The rest was easy.

It's just the first million or so that's hard to earn — and I'd done that by the time I turned twenty-three."

Hayely studied him with respect. It amazed her that this big body with its callused hands and beard stubble had such a brilliant and wise soul hidden inside it. He wasn't the money-hungry executive ogre she'd thought he was at the start of their deal.

On impulse, she reached up and ran her fingers carefully down the side of his face. It was too late to fire her at this late stage in the game and she wanted to touch him the way a friend might. His sweet self-confidence calmed her to the core. If he could flourish in an orphanage, there was no way she wouldn't survive an issue so insignificant as Kathy Mark.

"Thank you, Gary," she whispered. "No one else could have made me feel better." She leaned forward on impulse and shyly kissed his cheek.

Gary sat back in shock. "I don't know what I did, but whatever it was, it must have worked — because you're smiling again."

CHAPTER SIX

Hayely rolled over in bed and stretched like a sleek housecat in the early sunlight. The morning had come all too soon for her taste. She'd called in sick the night before, leaving a voicemail to say she wouldn't be coming in to the office. Why should she bother? She already knew her days were numbered, and she didn't plan to return until she had just the right resignation speech scripted out for her soon-to-be ex-boss.

Besides, the Chamber of Commerce Spring Banquet was that evening and she wanted to spend the day relaxing and getting ready for it at leisure. Several times she'd peeked into her closet at the dress that hung there. Every time she saw it, she felt like Cinderella going to the ball. Even though she'd been to a few ornate parties, she didn't think she'd ever owned a gown quite that dazzling in her life.

She pulled a cover up over her when she

heard a knock on the door. "Come in," she called out.

Gary opened the door and poked his head through. "I had a feeling you were sleeping in today." The cover slid off to one side and exposed one of her slender legs to his view and he quickly looked away. Then he looked back. A lot.

"I have to plan my great farewell speech for Ms. Mark, you know." She wasn't awake enough yet to notice the look in his eyes at first.

"Ah."

Then she noticed. It was as if nowhere he looked was right, and he didn't know where to rest his gaze. He could see the silky skin around her neck and collarbone now, too, and her glossy brown hair was wild around her, but she didn't change positions.

"Gary?"

"Be ready by six-thirty."

Hayely smiled as he shut the door. Was he as on edge as she was about the banquet that evening? After all, as soon as they arrived, the news would spread like wildfire and everyone in the city would know her as Mrs. Tarleton. She'd been very comfortable with her lifelong anonymity.

She crawled out of bed and walked into her bathroom in search of her toothbrush.

She'd never spent a day alone in the mansion before, but she'd filled it up with enough grown-up toys that she couldn't imagine anyone being bored there for even a minute.

There was an entire media room upstairs with a movie screen that slid down at the touch of a button. Next to the exercise room downstairs, there was a smaller room with a billiards table, dartboard and a shelf full of board games. But then, she might just curl up on the sofa and watch TV all day. The luxury of doing absolutely nothing was quite the temptation.

Still in her nightshirt, she walked leisurely down the halls. In another month, she'd have every room completely furnished, painted and arranged just so. The atmosphere definitely improved each week and Hayely was far ahead of schedule.

She went downstairs and looked into Gary's den. Had he brought in something new of his own? She stepped inside and crossed the room to the far wall for a better look. There in matching gold frames were three pictures hanging in a row. There was a photo of Gary and Charlie as boys standing together in front of a dilapidated car. Even so many years ago there was no mistaking their expressions — Gary with his serious scowl and Charlie with a wide grin that made his ears look too big for his head.

The next picture showed an elderly couple whom Hayely had never seen before. They were holding hands in front of a large hotel-like building and she supposed they had to be Mr. and Mrs. Bellmark. But the third picture was the one that startled her, the one she couldn't stop staring at. It was one of the shots taken in front of the fountain. The photographer had captured the two of them turned toward one another, his hand on hers, smiles lighting their eyes — who would ever guess they were only play-acting? Gary's hazel eyes even looked like those of a man deeply in love.

Hayely's own eyes misted over and she marched straight toward the kitchen, the place she felt most at home in the house. Out came the mixer, the cutting board and half a dozen random ingredients. Instinctively she chopped and stirred her way into a therapeutic calm. Cherry-chocolate éclairs was the solution for all her problems. Or so she wished.

She put down her spoon as tears threatened to well up again. "Nothing in my life is real right now," she said to herself as she looked around the big kitchen. "I think I might miss this place when I'm gone.

What's worse, I might even miss Gary."

She shook her head after venturing the words out loud. Lately it seemed that everything she said or thought made the reality of her situation more solid and terrifyingly real. She'd fooled herself into thinking her emotional struggles had been entirely caused by an uncertain career path, when the truth was that Kathy Mark didn't concern her nearly as much as she had anticipated. A career would come. Her thoughts were on Gary for the moment, and she had the fleeting feeling that life was passing her by while she did her best to be straight-laced and professional.

After a while, she put the éclairs into the refrigerator and headed back upstairs to get ready for the banquet. She lighted a large vanilla-scented candle on the edge of her bathtub and turned on the water into the shiny porcelain and gold oval. She hadn't done much to decorate this particular bathroom, but it was next on her list. She tugged her nightshirt off over her head and slipped into the water. It was only a little after noon and she could soak like this for hours if she liked. She didn't even bother to turn on the bathroom lights. Let the candlelight lull everything bad away, she thought as she closed her eyes.

■ ■ ■ ■

Downstairs, Gary clicked the front door shut and flung his boots with the round laces scattering messily into a corner. He couldn't think of the last time he hadn't worked straight through lunch, but he couldn't get Hayely's image to leave him alone. He almost couldn't sleep at night knowing she was in the next room. Sure, he could eat — she saw to that with all her amazing recipes, but sleep was out of the question.

All he did the night before was toss and turn, and she might as well have been a million miles away as just on the other side of that wall. The whole thing was maddening. He had never had time for this kind of distraction, much less met a woman who could hold his interest long.

He'd even asked her to stay on after the six months were up, and she'd rejected his offer without even giving it a thought. But then the next day she'd turned to him for reassurance and even let him comfort her. He couldn't understand her for the life of him.

He breathed in the air around him and knew she'd been baking again. But there

125

weren't any lights on in the house. Maybe she'd gone on in to work after all. For Hayely's sake, he hoped not. Gary jogged up the staircase toward his room.

The door to Hayely's room stood wide open. He almost passed by, but then he thought he saw something flicker, something beckoning to him in the mirror above her dressing table. A candle burning in the adjoining bathroom cast its reflection through the open door and into the mirror. And there was just enough light to illuminate the bathtub it sat on.

Gary couldn't breathe. He couldn't think. He couldn't even move for fear Hayely would notice him. All he could do was stare into the ornate glass at the vision it held. Hayely's brown hair floated loosely in the water around her shoulders. Her head rested against the back slope of the tub and her long eyelashes fluttered against her cheeks. Thousands of bubbles hid the rest of her from view, and she giggled as one of them fell through the air and landed on her nose.

He tiptoed slowly back the way he'd just come. He would be late for his hair appointment if he didn't leave now anyway. And it wouldn't do Hayely a bit of good to think he'd been spying on her. But it had done him good. Every time he saw her, he saw something new in her to think about.

Hayely's grey eyes fluttered open at the creaking sound outside the door. She didn't move a muscle at first and then slowly pulled the plug on the bathtub. She'd been thinking of Gary even though she thought she shouldn't. Was he really there? No, he couldn't be.

She took a long time to blow her hair dry and then brought it up into a sophisticated twist high on her head. She'd found some tiny hairpins with pearls attached to the top. When she held her hair in place with them, all anyone could see was a delicate interlacing of pearls against her rich brunette hair.

She took the dress off its hanger and stretched it out across the bed. It was the white-gray color of moonlight captured in a fine chiffon-like fabric she'd never seen before. Satiny royal blue flowers flowed down the material, demanding to be shown off during a warm spring evening.

Hayely picked up the dress and held it against her in front of the mirror. The halter style top would fasten behind her neck with three slick blue buttons and cause the fabric to fold in soft, low waves across her chest while leaving her arms completely bare.

Her back would also be exposed. She'd never been bold enough to wear a backless gown before. It was cut out all the way to a scoop below her waistline just before it found her curves and glided sleekly the rest of the way down to her ankles.

The clerk, Carla, had talked her into a satin choker necklace and elbow-length blue satin gloves that matched the shade of the tiny flowers in her dress. Pure glamour, Hayely thought, pure Cinderella secretary going to the ball with her handsome construction worker prince. Fitting. It was all a fairy tale anyway. At the stroke of midnight, or six months in her case, everything would change.

When she'd procrastinated long enough, she slipped into the dress and buttoned those three little buttons at the back of her neck. She tucked her feet into a pair of strappy little royal blue shoes with what she thought was a very trendy heel. With a tug and a snap, the necklace and gloves were in place.

She inhaled deeply, loving the way the faintest shadow of cleavage showed over the folds of fabric when she did. She left the room that was still hers for a while longer, and descended the staircase with great care not to catch her hem under a heel. When she looked up, she saw that her deliberate pace had been well worth it.

Charlie and Gary both stood at the bottom of the stairs in their tuxes, looking ready to whisk her away to the banquet. She smiled at Charlie first and then turned her attention to Gary. He was freshly shaven and his hair had been trimmed shorter in a new cut that was very, very attractive on him. Without all the usual stubble and grime, the god-like planes of his face were even more captivating than in the picture she'd seen on the Internet.

"Wow," was all Gary could say. Hayely really did look like a movie star from days gone by. Her bare skin glowed where she must have rubbed some kind of shimmery lotion into it, something that smelled divinely of sweet spring flowers. And that berry-colored lipstick stained her mouth a particularly kissable shade in his opinion.

Charlie elbowed him and said, "You look stunning, Hayely. You'll turn the whole town on its ear tonight." He elbowed Gary again. "Say something," he encouraged.

"Wow." Gary caught Hayely's gloved hands in his. He grinned proudly at Charlie. "To all of society, this is my wife."

Gary placed his warm hand at the small

of her back and led her outside to where a shiny black limo awaited the three of them. Seated closely beside her, Gary held onto Hayely's hand tightly as the limo moved smoothly over the driveway pavement and out onto the road.

Charlie watched the two closely. There was no doubt in his mind; Gary and Hayely had something passing between them that had nothing to do with business. Hayely couldn't stop touching Gary, whether a fingertip on his arm or her knee resting beside his leg, the contact was never broken.

When Charlie had first met Gary in the orphanage, he knew he'd behaved like nothing better than a scraggly, red-haired tagalong. But in no time flat, Gary had informed him he'd seen Charlie's gift for details and wanted him to run a corporate office one day.

That was Gary's gift — giving people self-respect, security and a sense of purpose. It was high time someone could return the favor to him. He just had to wonder if Gary would recognize the opportunity even if she walked down the stairs and into his limo.

"Are you ready for the big public appearance?" Charlie asked at last. "The great unveiling?"

Gary nodded. "What's in the old bag of

tricks for this year?"

Charlie laughed. "I don't know how we're going to top last year's pink fiasco. Maybe this year I'll tell them all you like women who really know how to slather on the make-up. Or, you know, I'll bet we could triple Nevada's cosmetic surgery market with a single comment."

Hayely looked at Charlie in shock as she realized the impact of their practical jokes. "You guys are terrible. You'll have the whole town scraping off eye shadow with chisels by next year's banquet. And I don't even want to think about that other inspiration you just had."

Gary squeezed her hand again. "Just a guess here, but I think the news of our marriage is probably going to be enough entertainment for this year."

The limo pulled up at the guest entrance to the hotel at which the event was always held. Coming in through the side door gave the appearance of a much lower-key evening than Hayely knew awaited them. That illusion was shattered as Hayely, Gary and Charlie handed away their coats and walked inside a ballroom artistically converted for the occasion.

At the head of the room, a long table set

up for the Chamber of Commerce officers sat empty except for a few well-placed microphones and crystal pitchers of water with condensation rolling down the sides. Flowers cascaded from corners and pillars. Ice sculptures glistened on the hors d'oeuvres tables. The great remainder of the room was speckled with round tables draped in, white linen, but there seemed to be no particular assigned seating.

At the back of the room around the dance floor and near the bar, hundreds of people mingled, talked and sipped from champagne flutes. Others sat here and there at some of the empty tables.

"I'll go on in and grab us a table," Charlie said.

Hayely rested her hand on Gary's arm in her best imitation of a wifely gesture. "You go on ahead, too. I'm going to visit the restroom first. I'll find you."

Gary nodded and followed Charlie to a table with a mediocre view of the main table. They didn't want to be too conspicuously up front in case they found a way to slip out early. Charlie ordered a glass of wine from a waiter as his friend sat down beside him.

"So have you told her your feelings for

her aren't so businesslike?" Charlie asked quietly.

"I have no idea what you're talking about."

"And have you asked her to forget that insane agreement and try being with you just because she wants to?"

"There's nothing going on, Charlie. You're pushing your luck again." Gary paused for a moment in thought. "Actually I did ask her to stay past the six months and she said no."

"You did? And she what?"

Gary's voice got even lower. "Apparently she doesn't want to become an interior designer."

"You mean you sounded like a boss extending an employee's contract," Charlie said flatly.

"What more could I do? It's a touchy situation. She could sue me if I cross the line. Or go to the media."

"Aw, come on. I've never heard anything more ridiculous come out of your mouth." Charlie paused as Gary looked at him. "Don't try that Tarleton glare with me. I'm the only one around you who'll tell it to you straight and so I'm going to. You're going to let something precious slip by if you don't wake up and pursue it."

"This isn't the place for this discussion.

Someone could overhear you." But Charlie's words nagged at him. They mingled with the memory of the brief kiss on their wedding day, the image of Hayely's skin glistening in the bathtub, the sound of his heart thudding in anticipation of her hand touching his arm throughout dinner.

As soon as Charlie and Gary settled into their seats, the crowd at the fringe of the room seemed to shift. Suddenly, all the tables around the two men filled with guests. Had they actually been waiting to see where Gary Tarleton would sit before choosing seats of their own? Gary flinched and ordered a cup of coffee just as he saw a flashbulb go off from somewhere across the room. As he set the cup down, the intrusive flash from an unseen camera went off again.

"Let the festivities begin," he muttered dimly and looked back to the doorway for some sign of Hayely.

Hayely emerged from the ladies room and wove her way through the crowd. The amount of people in the ballroom had increased greatly in only a few moments and the scattered tables that had been empty before she'd left Gary's side were now filled. A trio of violinists stood at the back of the room playing a soothing tune and the volume of laughter and animated discussions rose considerably.

"Excuse me," she said more than once as she turned first one way and then the next. Where was he anyway? Maybe Charlie's thick red hair would be easiest to spot. She stopped and scanned the room before ducking past another cluster of guests.

As Hayely took another careful step, the crowd parted slightly in front of her. There, standing right before her eyes, was the one person she hadn't considered running into — Kathy Mark. From the look on her boss's face, she'd seen Hayely as well. Sternly, critically, the older woman inspected Hayely's expensive gown as if mentally picking it apart seam by seam.

Kathy approached Hayely with a frozen smile on her face, but there was no mistaking the absolute rage in her pale blue eyes. "What the hell do you think you're doing here?" she demanded through a frozen smile.

Hayely was stunned, temporarily at a loss. "I'm going inside to the banquet." Where was that speech she'd started rehearsing in her head? She couldn't remember a word of it. All that bubbled into her mind were words too foul to say aloud in polite society. And where was Gary? If ever a rescue was in order, it was now.

Kathy stepped toward Hayely and her anemic yellow satin suit rustled as she moved. "I did not invite you to attend with K. L. Mark Enterprises. We are well represented by professionals who won't embarrass us. How dare you show up uninvited?"

Hayely looked up behind Kathy. Darryl stood sheepishly a few steps behind his mother. A gold chain showed underneath his partially opened tuxedo shirt and the heavy scent of aftershave couldn't hide that he'd already become well acquainted with the bar. He shoved his hands in his pockets and tried desperately not to look at anything other than his shoes.

Next to her brother, Dee looked torn between making a bawdy joke and taking a step forward to stand beside Kathy. She shifted uncomfortably in a knee-length black and white sequined swing dress that fit too snugly through her broad shoulders. Her sandy blonde hair now had short bangs that were striped with whitish highlights. Guess she found her way to the hairdresser, Hayely noted grimly.

"I'm not here for K. L. Mark," Hayely said with a great deal of calm in her voice. From the outside, she appeared unruffled and confident with her head held high when she spoke. Her uncomplicated beauty had already caught the attention of several people in the room, and they all turned to watch with interest at what was obviously a confrontation in the making.

"No, you most certainly are not," Kathy interrupted with a tone reminiscent of a hiss. "I can't believe I ever hired someone of your incompetence."

Hayely folded her hands neatly in front of her, the blue gloves lending a manner of poise to her stance. "As I was saying, I'm here with my husband."

"Your husband?" Kathy nearly snorted as she opened up her mouth to say something cruel. Hayely fully expected to hear the words "you're fired." She could almost see them hanging in the air attached to a cartoon balloon over Kathy's head when the woman's expression suddenly changed and her mouth snapped shut. In place of the villainess Hayely knew so well, appeared a simpering woman who all at once batted her lashes and gestured with great lightness.

As Gary took his place near Hayely's side, a hush ripped through the crowd. "Something wrong?" His glittering hazel eyes bored into Kathy's washed-out grey-blue ones.

Kathy smiled sweetly and flitted her hand

in the air toward him. "No. It's just that decent people are so hard to find these days. You know how it is, don't you, Gary?"

Hayely virtually held her breath. Should she say something? No, she didn't need to. Gary would tell Kathy what he thought of her, what they both thought of her. Maybe he'd turn and declare to the whole party all the shady things he knew about Kathy's business practices. Then the realization stuck Hayely — no one at the office had any idea that Gary Tarleton was her Gary. Even Kathy hadn't put two and two together yet.

With a smug smirk, Gary slid his powerful arm around Hayely and pulled her close to his side. The lustrous metal of his wedding band shone with an unabashed gleam on his hand as he ran his fingers smoothly down her bare upper arm and back to her shoulder. Hayely leaned securely against her husband, her curves fitting into his masculine angles so perfectly that the connection was obvious. The hush that had previously taken the room now shifted to a high-pitched dissonance of understanding.

Kathy's smile fell sickeningly from her face and her eyes widened, then narrowed just as quickly. She took a single step backward as the horror of the situation drifted over her. Hayely felt as if she were watching her boss's reaction in slow motion. Then with amazing calculation and control, Kathy replaced her mask of amiability.

"I was speaking of someone else of course. We love our Hayely, don't we?" She turned toward Darryl and Dee who nodded enthusiastically in support.

Without a sound, Gary turned Hayely toward him. She saw outright amusement in his eyes before he kissed her softly on the lips for all to witness and guided her away toward their table.

"See. Who needs words?" he asked with a roguish grin.

Hayely released her breath. "That was priceless. Thank you." She couldn't express the warmth and appreciation she felt under the protection of Gary's public support. But then, she wouldn't have expected anything less from him. Honorable to the core.

Gary and Hayely joined Charlie at the table just as dinner arrived. Waiters suddenly covered the room, working in efficiently orchestrated rows to place a meal on a white china plate in front of each guest.

"But why didn't you yell at her? Or tell her off?" Hayely asked quietly. If her father had been in Gary's place, she was sure his not-so-dulcet tones would have been heard for blocks.

"Why didn't you?" he countered with curiosity in his voice.

"I just couldn't. I wanted to hurt her, to get revenge somehow, but I just couldn't. Not even to her, especially in public."

"So you took the high road. She wouldn't have," Gary assured. "The path she's on leads nowhere. Let her walk straight into her demise all by herself. You've done all you could to get along with her in that office. Let it go."

Hayely bit into her bland chicken and swallowed thoughtfully. "What am I going to do now? I don't have a job."

Charlie took a swig of wine. "Easy. Cook, decorate, swim — whatever you want until you figure out what sort of career to start."

"You make it sound so simple," she said.

"It should be. I don't think Gary minds a bit if his wife works."

Gary glared at him and whispered, "Of course, you could also stay on with me past the six months."

Hayely smiled wistfully and sawed off another bite of chicken. To listen to Charlie talk, a person might think she and Gary had a chance at something. Their act had fooled even him on some level. After looking around the room, who there would guess that she and Gary would live together, laugh together from time to time — all for just a matter of a few more weeks.

"Hey, congratulations, buddy." A man Hayely had never seen before patted Gary vigorously on the back. "I had no idea you'd tied the proverbial knot. Way to go." He walked away after winking at Hayely.

"Who was that?" she asked.

"No idea. Might be a salesman I met last year. Don't worry, you get used to that sort of thing after a while."

As the meal wound down and people felt free to move around again, the line finding its way toward Gary and Hayely grew. Hayely didn't recognize anyone. She was in a room full of strangers who all seemed to know her.

"Congratulations, Mr. and Mrs. Tarleton."

"What wonderful news."

"I'm so happy for you."

Hayely found herself receiving handshakes and hugs as if she were in the reception line at a wedding. The screech of a microphone being dragged along the front table brought the socializing to a slow halt.

The members in charge of the local Chamber of Commerce took their places at the front of the room. Someone repeatedly clinked the edge of a butter knife against one of the crystal pitchers until the guests settled back into their seats. With the attention directed toward him, the president pulled the microphone up higher as he stood.

He said, "Before we start the awards ceremony, I think we have some special news to announce. It seems while we weren't looking, someone near and dear to us, a favorite past Chamber president no less, went off and got himself hitched. Gary and Hayely, why don't you stand up?"

Gary stood, pulled Hayely's chair back and helped her proudly from her seat. *Here you go, Nevada — my wife,* he thought. The more he thought the word, the more intimidating it sounded to him. Then an entire lifetime with Hayely stretched out ahead of him for just the blink of an eye, and the thought startled him.

Together they smiled and nodded to the room.

"Ladies and gentleman, I'd like to present Mr. and Mrs. Gary Tarleton!"

His heart filled his chest to capacity. The announcement. Those words. They felt perfectly right somehow.

The room erupted in applause and whistles

before the evening became a complete blur for Hayely. Everything happened happily and fast in the ballroom. All the awards were given out before she knew it, and she could hardly smile enough when Gary's firm walked away with Business of the Year.

True to form, his acceptance speech was brief and humble, but Hayely could have wept when his appreciative gaze never once strayed from her as he spoke. She didn't see how anyone else in the room could have missed it either.

With the golden plaques distributed, everyone moved to the dance floor and the bar. She encountered people of all motivations as she mingled through the crowd with Gary, once again giving her best impersonation of a wife. Some people shot her looks of open jealousy. Others seemed genuinely pleased about their marriage. But most assessed Gary as if he were a commodity. She thought he deserved so much more.

When they neared the edge of the crowd, Gary let go of her hand and his fingertips slid down Hayely's palm as they lost contact. Yet something else connected in that moment and Gary turned to look down at Hayely. There was a gleam in his eyes that told her volumes when she met his gaze.

For a minute, the crowd seemed to fade

and all that was left was the realization of the very real, heated fascination that passed between her and this beautiful man who didn't look at all as if he were pretending.

"Hayely —" he began and then didn't seem to know what to say.

"Let's go home," she whispered into his ear. "Haven't we put in enough of an appearance?"

If it weren't for his keen instincts where character was concerned, Hayely couldn't imagine how Gary could exist in such an assemblage. Would they have gravitated toward him so if he were only a middleclass construction worker? She knew she would. With one look at him, she knew she would. The blatant desire in his eyes sent a ripple through her.

For the time that passed during that look, Hayely and Gary shoved the world away. He took her hand again as they made their way to the exit.

On their way out the door, Charlie took on an impish look. "I can't resist," he warned his companions. He leaned slightly out of his way to catch Kathy's attention as she gossiped with a friend near the door. "Please see that Mrs. Tarleton's final paycheck is sent to the house," he said brightly to her, loving the emphasis he placed on the two words that would undoubtedly set Kathy's teeth on edge.

Without waiting for a response, Hayely, Gary, and Charlie headed home.

CHAPTER SEVEN

When they arrived at the mansion the night before, Hayely had been exhausted in the utterly complete way only wrought emotions can bring.

Her entire life was changing from week to week, and her situation had improved slightly in her estimation. At least now she'd gotten rid of the thing she didn't want — a job she loathed. Only now she was left missing what she wanted, and that wasn't simply a career calling anymore. Her pretend marriage to Gary weighed heavily on her. The night before, their interaction had felt so comfortable, so vibrantly real that it was easy sometimes to forget the nature of their six-month relationship.

After the banquet, Hayely had fallen into bed exhausted. If only she could erase her recollection of him asking her to stay on as an employee after the six months were up. He'd been honest about his expectations all along. Was it too late to want more? She doubted a little shared time alone would take his original intentions and flip them one-hundred-and-eighty degrees.

Well into mid-morning, Hayely opened her eyes and knew she was alone in the big house. Gary was always awake with the dawn and gone to work before her own internal body clock stirred her. As she sat up, the entire Chamber of Commerce Banquet sprung to mind all in one quick memory. She moaned and then laughed out loud at the same time. There was no hiding it now — her secret was out. At least with no job to speak of, she didn't have to awaken to the ring of an annoying alarm clock.

Hayely padded downstairs in a pair of slippers that resembled stuffed teddy bears and picked yesterday's mail up from the table in the foyer. When had Gary added her name to everything? From bills to the newspaper, her name joined his on the label. Curious, she walked around the house surveying rooms. Just as she'd suspected, someone had hung up still more pictures of the two of them together — a large one in the living room and another in the unfinished library. The decorative frame stood out awkwardly beside the columns of empty bookshelves.

When the telephone rang, Hayely nearly jumped out of her slippers and her heart thudded wildly against her thick blue terry-cloth robe. In all the time she'd spent in the house, never once had she heard the phone ring.

"Hello?" she answered cautiously. Was she or wasn't she entitled to answer the phone in what the rest of the world thought was her own home? What was the correct proto-col?

"Hayely, it's me." Gary's voice rolled to her from across the line, caressing her all the way down to her toes just by speaking her name.

She breathed in to still the flutters in her chest. "You surprised me, Gary." She'd almost called him something like "honey" in return and thought the better of it.

"Should I come home for an early lunch?"

Hayely held the phone silently to her ear for just a moment. "Yes."

"I'll be there."

Hayely ran to the kitchen as fast as her teddy bear feet would allow. What could she find? Bacon and tomato sandwiches, French fries and a side salad would have to do on such short notice. She measured a scoop of lush smelling grounds into a filter and turned on the coffeemaker.

Hayely scrambled to find the drawer in which she'd accidentally put the tomatoes inside the massive refrigerator. With bacon sizzling in the frying pan and sourdough bread in the toaster oven, she'd have lunch ready in no time. But she'd witnessed Gary's lead foot and knew the office wasn't too far down the freeway from home. Quickly, she pulled the French fries out of the deep fryer before they turned one too many shades of golden brown.

Just as Gary walked into the kitchen, Hayely plunked down a plate full of food on the table. "Ta da!" she announced with a smile and a grand gesture.

She drew in a breath and looked up at him. His dark hair was styled neatly and barely a trace of stubble covered his chin, but the telltale signs of construction dust hung in his hair and on his shirt. Her heart made an out of synch thud just from the mere sight of him and the sensation stopped her in her tracks.

Gary approached the table slowly and without even glancing down at his food, growled, "I think I might have to make it a to-go order. We need to talk."

Hayely blushed furiously as the reason for his visit home came to her. Last night. He remembered that look just as vividly as she did. She tugged the belt to her robe a little tighter around her and sat down. She was in the middle of the kitchen in broad daylight wearing nothing but a robe and a pair of not-so-attractive slippers.

"I should have gotten dressed, but I was in a hurry."

"So was I."

Gary slid his chair closer to Hayely until he could see every tiny thing about her face. With her disheveled hair and eyes still bright from sleep, she looked more attractive to him than ever. That she had settled into this home so easily brought him a joy he hadn't noticed before. She just seemed to fit.

"Hayely," he said as he toyed with the ends of her bathrobe belt and pulled her closer to him. "My pretty Hayely." He bent nearer, the look in his eyes telling her that the kiss he intended to give her would be nothing like the harmless ones he'd given before.

Hayely senses spun. She wanted the kiss. She did. But for the first time, the term "marriage of convenience" rang true on an entirely different level to her and that level troubled her. Oh, but she wanted that kiss.

Hayely put her hand against Gary's chest.

Should she push him away? Try to go back to the way things were before? Just as she had decided, the noise of the front door opening took the need for action away from her.

Charlie sauntered into the kitchen with a newspaper curled under his arm. "Nice bear feet," said as he tossed the paper onto the table. "I tried to call, but you had your cell phone off. What gives?"

Gary growled, "You'd think that would be a hint." He poured himself a cup of coffee and crossly sat down in front of his lunch.

"Look at this." Charlie looked from Gary to Hayely, shrugged as if some great meaning had been lost on him, and feigned that he had noticed nothing. He opened the newspaper to the society section and tapped the pictures there for emphasis.

Hayely leaned slightly over Gary's shoulder. "Oh my." Her hand fluttered to her mouth as she read.

There, on the first page of the section, were pictures of her dancing with Gary, standing with Gary as the Chamber of Commerce president announced their marriage, and a larger professional shot of the two of them that looked suspiciously like one the photographer they'd hired must have taken in the garden.

Gary scanned through the accompanying article. "They didn't waste any time, did they? Sure did their research."

"How did they find out my parents' names?" she asked in bewilderment. "They even have my age and where I'm from."

"Reporters," Charlie answered. "It doesn't take a lot of effort for them to dig up a person's background. Lucky you're not a criminal or they'd be all over that, too." He winked at Hayely playfully.

"We need to talk to your parents," Gary said matter-of-factly. "I've been looking forward to meeting my new contract in-laws anyway. No time like the present."

Charlie closed the newspaper and handed it to Hayely. "I imagine you'll want to keep this." He wondered if fifty years down the road, they would look at that newspaper and treasure it.

Hayely's throat choked shut. What would her father say? And her poor mother? At least the chances of them finding out about the nature of the business arrangement were slim. They'd just believe she'd gotten married. Straightforward as that. But the thought of facing them so soon — maybe they didn't know. Maybe they hadn't seen anything in the media. Maybe she could stay happily in her cocoon of denial and put off talking to them just a while longer.

Charlie turned to Gary. "The real reason I wanted to reach you on your cell was that you got a call at the office a little while ago. Just after you took off in such a hurry."

Gary stuffed several fries in his mouth and chewed, raising his eyebrows questioningly in response. "And?"

"Mr. Bellmark says he and his wife are coming to town. Tonight," Charlie stated with emphasis. "I haven't seen them in so long," he added with a wisp of nostalgia in his voice.

"Tonight?" Hayely asked. She'd barely had time to consider breaking the controversial news of their marriage to her parents and now this? She'd have to work fast to get their guest bedroom ready. The rest of the place was looking respectable enough for visitors. She wouldn't have time to cook, though. Maybe they could all go out to a restaurant. Being a pretend wife sure carried with it enough of the responsibilities of a real marriage.

Gary downed the rest of his coffee and stood quickly. "I'll see you tonight after I pick the Bellmarks up from the airport. We'll have that discussion later." He gave Hayely's hand a squeeze on impulse before striding in long steps out of the house to his truck.

"How big is your car, Charlie?" Hayely asked, her gaze following Gary out the door.

"I've got one of the company trucks today. Why?"

"Perfect. My car doesn't have much in the way of a trunk, and I'm going to have to do some major shopping today to get the guest room ready. Actually, it's the bathroom I'm worried about. Feel like a trip into the city?"

Charlie's eyes twinkled as he looked down toward her feet. "I'll just pour myself a cup of coffee while you get ready."

"Thanks," Hayely yelled out behind her as she ran for the stairs.

In no time at all, Hayely and Charlie were on their way down the road. She remembered clearly how to find the boutique and directed Charlie that way. As the weeks went by, she found that she got lost in the city much less frequently and had even managed to accumulate some favorite stores.

"I've got to pick up a couple outfits I ordered. Want to wait for me?"

"Nah. I'll come in. I hate to just sit and wait."

When Hayely walked into the shop, Carla recognized her immediately and ran to greet her. "I've already heard the buzz. You must have been awesome. Everyone in here's been talking about you and Gary. They say he never takes his eyes off of you. Lucky girl."

Hayely smiled shyly. "I don't think I'll ever get used to people around here. I'm not sure why my life is that fascinating."

"Sure. Nothing out of the ordinary at all," Carla said sarcastically and made a light-hearted face. Then she looked up and grinned brilliantly as she noticed Charlie, her attention focusing completely away from Hayely. "I'm Carla." She stuck out her hand daringly to grab his.

Charlie turned crimson all the way down his fingertips. "I'm Charlie." He shook her hand with a mix of awkwardness and sincerity that appeared to catch Carla by surprise.

Hayely looked back and forth between the two of them, recognizing a spark when she saw it. "Carla," she interrupted, "can I get my order?"

Carla dropped Charlie's hand with a giggle and walked to a back room. She emerged with a heavy garment bag in her hand.

"We got in everything, made to fit. We have a couple ensembles that would work for entertaining at home in the evening, that other formal gown you picked out, and two casual daytime outfits. Oh, and in this other bag are the shoes and hat you liked."

"That's exactly right," Hayely confirmed. Her insides tightened as she mentally tallied the cost of her purchase. Her last month's paycheck would cover some of it, and she was sure she could earn the rest later. She couldn't think of a way to avoid the expense; she had nothing appropriate to wear in Gary Tarleton's world. She signed the credit card slip with her new name, a name she was quickly becoming used to seeing everywhere she looked.

Hayely thanked Carla and smiled when she saw the salesclerk hand Charlie a business card on the way out the door. Hayely was even more tickled when he dug out one of his own and traded Carla for it.

Charlie shut the truck door after Hayely hopped inside and positioned himself behind the wheel. "Charlie and Carla. Nice ring to it."

Hayely punched him lightly on the shoulder. "If I'm right, she wrote her home phone number on the back. You ought to give her a call."

"That, I might." He blushed scarlet again underneath his light smattering of freckles. His bright blue eyes with long curled lashes were definitely his most striking feature next to his richly hued hair, Hayely assessed. With his pleasant mouth and well-shaped face, she thought he just might have a chance with Carla.

Hayely turned away from Charlie and tucked the receipt into her purse, making a noise of dread as she did. "I'll have to let Gary know I'll pay him back for the clothes." She grimaced. "I shouldn't have spent so much."

Charlie laughed oddly. "Very funny."

Then he looked at her expression and wondered if she had a dry sense of humor that he hadn't noticed before. She certainly seemed serious, but Charlie shook the feeling aside. He didn't have Gary's knack for reading people he didn't know well quickly. The idea that Gary would want Hayely to reimburse him for anything was laughable. If anything, the man who was his boss and best friend wished Hayely would accept more from him if that silver car were any indication.

Hayely looked at Charlie as if he'd turned green, but decided not to say anything. She didn't really know him well enough to understand what he'd meant by "very funny." Of course she was responsible and would repay her debts. She wouldn't be in the situation she was in if those morals weren't ingrained in her nature in the first place.

Hayely spent the next three hours running Charlie ragged — but he seemed to be such a willing victim that she decided to use it her own advantage. From one store to the next, she added bag after bag to Charlie's arms until they finally had to return to the truck to toss it all inside.

"I think I've about worn out the poor credit card. Good thing its use will expire in three months or we'd have to replace it," Hayely joked.

Charlie frowned and rubbed his aching, shopping-fatigued arms. She apparently didn't know that Gary had asked him to request a new card for her, one that wouldn't expire for at least the standard two years.

"I'll have to look into that," he said in all earnestness. He wondered if Gary was finally coming to his senses.

Hayely barely had enough time to get everything done. She'd sent Charlie to set out everything they'd bought in the guest bathroom. From plush towels and bathmats to intricately carved guest soaps and ritzy shampoos, she'd asked him to line the marble countertops with these things and a smattering of flowers as if the room belonged to a five-star hotel.

Charlie was even in charge of putting the luxurious new bedding on the bed. For good measure she added houseplants and candles around the bedroom to make it seem homier for the Bellmarks. Their visit couldn't be more important to Gary, she reasoned.

With Charlie occupied, Hayely immediately dove into her work in the kitchen. She had wine, soda, bottled water, juices — whatever she guessed the older couple might want. She dipped fresh strawberries in chocolate, stuffed a couple dozen big mushrooms, and set out some cheese and crackers. It certainly wasn't a spread she'd call her best work, but it would have to do on such short notice.

Still on the run, Hayely jumped in a steaming hot shower and stood there letting the water flow over her. Had she found a chance to relax even a little bit all day? At least she was earning her keep, she reasoned.

Hayely dried off and walked into the dressing room between the master bedroom and bath to make sure everything looked all right. She'd decorated the area with only him in mind, and hoped he wouldn't dislike the feminine touches she added. No one disliked fresh floral arrangements, did they?

Hayely buttoned up one of the shirts she'd picked up from the boutique just that day. With sleeves that came down only to her elbows and a collar that stood up just a little in back, Carla had tailored the mint green cotton exactly the way Hayely had envisioned.

She tucked the shirt into her new dress pants made of simple, black material that came up into a high-waisted design. Small slits in the flowing legs of her pants near her ankles matched those at the ends of her sleeves. Comfortable for home, but not too casual, she concluded as she turned around full circle in the mirror.

She almost ran into Gary as she left the dressing room. "I didn't know you were back." Her hand fluttered to her chest as her heart pounded a little faster with surprise — or something else.

"They're downstairs with Charlie," Gary breathed out. "I wanted to come up and get you. Their room looks great." He sat down on the edge of the bed and looked up at Hayely.

"Charlie put in a lot of the labor."

Hayely was sure her insides went through a meltdown as she returned his gaze. Here was a man with one of the most naturally muscular physiques she'd ever seen, and he was looking up at her with something akin to childlike terror in his eyes. She sat down beside him and took his big hand reassuringly in her own.

"The dream that drove me since childhood rides on this visit, Hayely. I have to make sure those kids get the same chance I was given."

"You're a good man, Gary Tarleton. I just know that as soon as you tell the Bellmarks about your plans, they'll let you buy it from them. I'm sure they don't want to see it closed any more than you do. It's been their whole lives' work, hasn't it?"

Gary smiled, his teeth looking whiter than ever under his growing stubble. "That's what I keep telling myself." He twisted to the side and reached into the pocket of his khaki trousers. "I bought these for you. I saw the hairpins you used and thought — well, here." He handed her a small black box.

Hayely pulled the lid open and looked back up at Gary. "You don't need to keep buying me things, Gary. I don't expect that. I don't need it."

"I know. And that's exactly why I do it." He plucked the intricately strung pearl earrings from their velvet case and let them dangle from between his finger and his thumb. "They'll look good with what you have on."

Hayely put on the earrings and took his hand for him to lead her downstairs. She couldn't help but think of all the ways he made her feel treasured. It was ironic that such a blessing could be designed so temporary.

Seated on the cozy sofa Hayely had chosen were their first guests. She was relieved that Charlie had thought to build a fire in the fireplace. The blaze added an ambience that nothing artificial could duplicate.

"Mr. and Mrs. Bellmark," Gary said, "this is my beautiful bride, Hayely." He almost made the charade sound sincere.

Hayely liked them immediately, though the image she'd had of them was nothing close to reality. At nearly eighty years of age, Mrs. Bellmark wore her long white hair up in a ponytail and her clothes in a youthful fashion. Decked out jeans, a scarlet red sweatshirt, and trendy tennis shoes, she didn't seem to have lost much of her vitality over the years. Hayely suddenly felt close to overdressed for the evening.

Mr. Bellmark surprised her almost as much. He wore tan cowboy boots, jeans, and a black polo shirt. He was shorter and thinner than he appeared in the picture Gary had placed on the wall of his den — and much less stuffy.

"Very nice to meet you both," Hayely greeted.

She tilted her head toward the kitchen so that Charlie would take the hint and run to get the trays of finger foods she'd thrown together. Already she saw they had full cups of hot tea on the coffee table in front of them. She couldn't imagine Gary having made tea — Charlie must have come to the rescue again.

Mrs. Bellmark rose to her feet and caught up both of Hayely's hands in hers. "Well, you sweet thing. I can see why Gary chose you. But for the life of me —"

"I can't see what you saw in him," Mr. Bellmark finished his wife's sentence with a hearty laugh. "Relax, Gary. It was a joke," he said before turning back to Hayely. "He always was too serious — even as a boy."

Charlie returned and plunked the hors d'oeuvres trays down on the coffee table. "I'll bet you're starved after such a long trip?" He sank into a plush gold-toned chair as the couple sat back down on the sofa, and Gary and Hayely found a place on the loveseat nearby.

"Actually," Mrs. Bellmark said, "we ate on the plane coming in. No need to worry about dinner just because of us."

"And no need to get down to business right off the bat, either," Mr. Bellmark added. "We've got a couple days before we need to think about any of that."

Hayely nodded, "I agree. Do you have any plans for tomorrow? Or can we show you the sights? We have an amazing exercise room and swimming pool right here in the house. I haven't spent much time there, but there are stables out back, too. We could go horseback riding?" she offered enthusiastically.

Gary squeezed Hayely's hand tighter and didn't even seem to notice that he was toying with her wedding ring. "Is there anything you wanted to see in town? Somewhere we could take you?"

"No, dear," Mrs. Bellmark said. "I think we'd just enjoy sleeping in late, walking through that enormous garden I saw, and getting reacquainted. The horses sound nice. A little shopping couldn't hurt either." She gave Hayely a conspiratorial wink.

"I'd like a tour of your company," Mr. Bellmark added.

So would I, Hayely thought. Why hadn't she asked Gary to show her around his office before? She would have looked much more prepared that way, and it seemed as if she would need all her wits about her to help Gary through the next few days. He had grown so tense beside her that she could almost feel his nervous anxiety soaking through her skin.

Charlie stood up slowly and stretched the kinks out of his back. "I hate to leave so soon, but I have to get up early for work tomorrow so that I can leave early."

Gary raised an eyebrow at his friend.

Charlie grinned. "I've got a date."

Hayely stood and clapped her hands together. "She said yes? Way to go, Charlie!"

Gary looked confused. "When did all this happen?"

Hayely rested her hand on Gary's arm. "Don't worry. I'll catch you up on everything."

Mr. Bellmark rose to his feet and helped his wife stand. "Better watch it," he said to Gary. "If you're lucky, she'll be running circles around your life in no time."

Gary gazed with admiration at Hayely. "I hope so."

Hayely knew she looked startled and composed herself quickly. Sometimes he was too good of an actor and she couldn't tell where make-believe ended and reality began.

As Gary finished up some business with Charlie out in the driveway, Hayely escorted their tired guests upstairs and shut the bedroom door softly behind them for the night. She walked back to the room she would have to share with Gary and unbuttoned her shirt carefully. Too bad she'd wasted one outfit for an hour's visit, she mused and arranged the mint green fabric carefully on its hanger.

Gary groaned when he walked into his bedroom and saw Hayely standing with her heavy bathrobe wrapped all the way around her up to the neck. He hadn't considered their sleeping arrangements with the Bellmarks in the house. He'd been too busy feeling so proud to have her on his arm in front of his guests. She'd been nothing short of loving toward the older couple. He couldn't wait to buy the boys' home, and now he was even curious to meet her possibly furious parents.

Hayely crossed her arms over her chest. "You should knock," she whispered adamantly.

"On my own bedroom door?" he whispered back huskily. His gaze shifted from

Hayely to the bed and back again.

When he didn't take a step toward her, she asked, "You're going somewhere, aren't you?"

"Do you want me to stay?" Gary tilted his head to the side and ran his hand along his scruffy chin.

"I —" she stammered.

"Don't worry. But this is going to make me look like a terrible husband in front of the Bellmarks. I've got to head back into the office for a few hours. Since I'm taking the next couple days off to be with our guests, I've got to take care of some things tonight. You and I still need to talk."

"When will you be home?"

He didn't know if she felt disappointment or relief in the realization that she'd probably be asleep long before he returned from the office.

"Late. Much later than I'd like. You shouldn't wait for me. I'm sorry. Time will be on our side soon enough."

As Gary left the room, Hayely sank down into the heavy feather-filled comforter alone on the big bed. Time on their side? Did he think she'd agree to keep up the charade longer now that she was unemployed? No — from the way she saw their situation, time was definitely against them. With only a couple months of security stretching ahead of her, a sense of dread was creeping over her a little more each day. In a matter of weeks, she'd have to leave Gary and this temporary home. If he felt the same stirrings she was feeling for him, he would have made it clear. And he hadn't.

Hayely was utterly and completely miserable by the time she drifted off into sleep.

As soon as they were firmly seated in their saddles, Mr. and Mrs. Bellmark grabbed the reins and took off atop their horses at a gallop. The powerful animals were Quarterhorses, and much too high strung for an elderly couple to be riding in Gary's opinion. Mrs. Bellmark's white ponytail whipped out behind her, bouncing along as her husband laughed at the sight and tried to catch up to her.

"Doesn't look like they're going to need any lessons," Hayely said. "Think we'll ever see them again? They'll be in California by tonight at that rate."

He smiled. "We're going to have to get more than two good riding horses," Gary observed. "Might even trade those two in. Never seemed like a priority until now."

"There's one more horse in the stables. At

least I think I saw a big black one in one of the stalls this morning."

"The Friesian? I suppose we could ride him together if you felt like it."

"Why don't we just wait for the Bellmarks?"

"Coward," Gary whispered. "You know, these horses were bred as war horses, big enough to carry both a knight and his armor into battle after traveling for weeks."

"But if he's too big for most people to ride easily, why did you want him?

"He fits me just fine in case you haven't noticed. Besides, once I see something I like, I generally don't let it go."

The Bellmarks circled back and stopped in front of Gary and Hayely. Mr. Bellmark called out, "Do you two want a turn? I think we're hogging the horses." His cheeks were stained a happy red from the brisk ride in the cool spring air.

Gary wrapped his arms around Hayely and squeezed her shockingly close against his body. "No, you two take all the time you want. Have fun. There's a trail that runs up the hills off the back of the property. See the gate there?"

"You're sure it's alright?" Mrs. Bellmark asked with just a hint of breathlessness in her voice.

"Come on, Hilda," Mr. Bellmark said with a chuckle, "Can't you see they'd rather be doing exactly what they're doing right now?"

"Ah, honeymooners," she sighed. "Remember those days, dear?"

"We'll just be inside fixing lunch," Hayely quickly clarified as she squirmed away from his embrace. "The man at the stables will take care of the horses, won't he Gary?"

Gary nodded. "Just drop them off and come inside when you're ready."

With a hearty laugh of understanding, the older couple turned their horses at a more leisurely pace than before in the direction Gary had pointed.

Hayely's nearness to him affected him more than he'd like to admit, and he hadn't missed her kindness toward the Bellmarks. He checked himself mentally. She was just doing her job. He held her hand anyway as they walked into the house together.

Hayely had almost finished cooking lunch by the time the Bellmarks walked inside after their horseback adventure. She would have had the meal prepared several minutes sooner if it hadn't been for Gary's meddling. Every time she turned around, she had to slap his hand away from some ingredient on the counter. His energy was impossible to repress whenever he seemed happy or determined.

She smiled up at him. Without his usual stern manner and scowl of seriousness, he looked like the strikingly handsome, energetic thirty-something man he truly was. When Mr. Bellmark finally came to the table after showering away a great deal of horse hair, Gary finally left Hayely's side and sat next to him. Hayely sighed and set the table around them.

Mrs. Bellmark came into the dining room with a book in her hands, its pages yellowing with age and held together by a large rubber band. Carefully, she removed the band and set the book down on the wide table in front of Hayely.

"I thought you two might like to look at pictures while we eat," she explained. "We kept regular pictures of Gary and Charlie for about seven years. Couldn't keep up with those two monkeys after that."

Hayely placed several hot dishes full of food onto potholders to avoid singeing the expensive and well-polished table she'd recently purchased for the dining room. In spite of the lesser accommodations, she realized that Gary and Charlie always seemed to wind up sitting with her at the tiny kitchen table. It was nice to have an excuse to use the big dining room table for once. She looked over Mrs. Bellmark's shoulder and recognized a picture on the first page.

"We have that one hanging up in the den," Hayely pointed out.

"That's the first one we ever took of Gary. It was right after he came to live with us."

Mr. Bellmark added, "He and Charlie were like two peas in a pod. Inseparable."

"Right through college," Mrs. Bellmark said. "They went to the same school only a year or so apart. Moved to the same town after that."

"He became my brother," Gary said. "I was lucky in the sense that I got to choose my family. Living with the two of you in the boys' home gave me chances at life that most kids in my position only dreamed of."

Mr. Bellmark put his gnarled hand on the younger man's shoulder. "I know you want to pass that gift along, Gary. I admire you for that."

"No business talk at the table," Mrs. Bellmark chastised.

Gary grimaced. "I remember that tone well."

For a while they ate and stayed safely in the realm of small talk until Mrs. Bellmark turned the page of the photo album again.

"See this group picture? We took this right after we opened our doors. What year was that anyway? I can't recall now. So many of them were just babies when they came to us."

Hayely saw loneliness and open fright in the eyes of the tiniest children, and a front of bravery in the picture of a ten-year-old Gary. He was one of the oldest there.

"I can't imagine growing up without my parents. They weren't always easy to live with but still —"

"Well, as soon as you and Gary have children, they'll have the best of lives. All the advantages. Have you thought about babies yet?" Mrs. Bellmark stopped talking and looked expectantly at Hayely for an answer.

Hayely looked fleetingly at Gary. He had stopped eating with his fork full of food suspended in mid-air as if her next words would chart the future of the universe. What would he have wanted her to say? They hadn't discussed the subject, so Hayely blurted out what was in her heart.

"I want children. I do. If I could plan out my life perfectly, I'd pick a career I could control, so that I can work out of the house and raise my babies. No daycare nightmares. No nannies with values that might not be like ours. Do you know what I mean?"

Where in the world had that answer come from? If she had looked up, she would have seen Gary beaming with an arrogantly pleased smile that threatened to split his handsome face.

Mrs. Bellmark nodded in deep agreement. "Gary, my boy, you have a wise young wife. Hayely, you're right. There's no more joy in the entire world than a good marriage and a bunch of fat healthy babies to call your own." She winked at her husband and tossed her white ponytail back over her shoulder.

"Did you ever have children? Other than the boys in the boys' home I mean?" Hayely asked with more interest than she now felt.

Mr. Bellmark nodded. "We started very young. Had two daughters almost fully grown by the time we opened the home."

Gary still hadn't stopped smiling as he silently lifted his fork to his mouth again. He shook his head and looked pleased if not bewildered.

Mr. Bellmark dabbed his chin with a napkin and set it down on the table. "Well, Hilda. About ready to take off?"

Hayely looked at Mr. Bellmark with an expression of dull surprise. "You're going somewhere?"

"We'll have a hot time on the old town tonight," the elderly couple both sang out in unison as if they'd practiced the line a hundred times before. Hayely looked with envy at their joy after so many decades together. That's what I want, she thought suddenly. That and nothing less.

An ache had begun in the center of her and she felt as if something vast had gone missing there. But that was ridiculous. If anything, she was closer to where she wanted to be than before, wasn't she? Maybe she would miss what Gary and his home had come to symbolize for her. He represented all the possibilities of all the things she wanted. It would be natural to miss that influence when it was gone.

Mrs. Bellmark tucked the album under her arm and they all walked to the front door together. "It's really been wonderful visiting with you," she said warmly. "See you early tomorrow then?"

Hayely nodded and responded with a smile that didn't reach her eyes, "Yes, tomorrow at the office."

Mr. Bellmark shook Gary's hand and gave Hayely a quick hug. "Take care of him," he instructed and turned to Gary. "And you take care of her. She's one of a kind."

Mr. Bellmark's kindness was nearly

Hayely's undoing. "Excuse me, but I just remembered something I have to check," she said and turned to leave before the Bellmarks could see the tears that threatened. "See you tomorrow morning," she called out.

Hayely walked quickly from the foyer and headed for Gary's den, the only room she could think of far enough away and insulated enough to hide the sound of her sobs from the departing guests. Suddenly and so unexpectedly, a wave of dark emotion nearly drowned her. Babies? She couldn't think of starting a family, couldn't consider the laughter of small children in the big house, especially couldn't let herself imagine a child with Gary's perfect cheekbones and her silver eyes. She wasn't acting any better than a schoolgirl writing her boyfriend's name after hers in her diary.

She was full of ridiculous thoughts. She and Gary weren't even romantically involved. A family life like that might never be hers. She suddenly thought of her arrangement with Gary and regretted it bitterly as the tears started to flow in earnest. No love, no real job, no real life, she thought. It was as if everything she'd ever wanted was always an inch away from her fingertips and she could never cross that tiny distance to grasp it.

Following discretely behind after a few minutes, Gary stepped into his den and reached back to lock the door behind him without taking his eyes off Hayely. He'd sent the Bellmarks on their way out to spend the evening at one of those luxury hotels they'd seen in a brochure, but not before Gary knew they'd sensed Hayely's distress.

"What's going on? I can't begin to understand what's happening inside that head of yours. You haven't acted the same for a couple days now. Not since the Banquet for sure."

Hayely's eyes glowed like hot mercury. "Why do you even care, Gary? Really. This is all just a big game to you anyway."

He studied her distraught face for a moment. "What in the world are you talking about?"

"This arrangement. This fake, hateful, horrible marriage. I thought I was strong. I thought I could agree to your terms. But I'm not doing very well at being professional. My feelings get in the way and it's terrible."

Gary's eyes swam with confusion. "You

hate me. You regret marrying me," he stated flatly.

Of course she did, he thought. How could he have expected her to completely brush aside the way he'd forced her to marry him in the first place? He'd planned on talking to her ever since that look passed between them at the Banquet. He'd thought he'd sensed the spark of something real. But mostly it seemed he'd been a fool to think he could overcome such a bad start in so little time.

"No, you big burly — architect," she spat when no insult would come quickly enough to mind. "What I regret," she said miserably, "is that I'm just a six-month convenience you're getting too used to, that's all."

"Just a convenience?" At least she didn't say she hated him. There was a chance still. Gary wanted to tell her that the agreement they'd signed was meaningless to him by the day and she was meaning more. How much more, he didn't know. But he wanted to find out.

And Hayely wanted to ask him if he had any idea how painful it is pretending for the entire world that she had something she didn't.

Instead they stood silently looking at one another.

"You just don't understand," she said.

Gary gathered Hayely into his arms. He was at a loss where such emotion was concerned, when a woman cried as if her heart were snapping in half. The time had come. He had to make sure she understood how he felt about her, make it clear how unbelievably stunning she had grown in his eyes.

"Hayely, I have to tell you something."

"I know. I'm terribly unprofessional. I've heard it before." She sniffled against his sleeve and then straightened. "What?"

"I do understand. I want you to stay past the six months."

Her silver eyes glimmered. "I've heard that song before, too."

"Ah hell." Gary pulled her close up against his broad chest. "Just stay."

Hayely wiped the remaining tears away, her eyes still bright. "You like me."

A touch of crimson stained his cheeks and he nodded.

"How much?" she asked.

With his hand resting gently on her cheek, he lowered his lips to hers. He caressed her softly at first and she gasped as his kiss invited her to open her heart to him.

Hayely was energized beyond reason. Never, never in her controlled life had a man's kiss sent her reeling into oblivion. She couldn't even pull a coherent protest together.

She stood up on her toes to reach him and twined her hands into his hair. The thought that she was kissing Gary Tarleton, her boss, crossed her mind but she didn't think to move away. She didn't think at all with his lips pressed against hers.

Gary had been kissed by women, many women whose touches stopped him cold almost instantly. He'd sensed the greed, the ulterior motives in them. But all he felt in Hayely's kiss was unbridled yearning. What he wouldn't give to do more. But there were limits, and this was all too new. Reluctantly, he ended the kiss.

"Why, Mrs. Tarleton, I had no idea." He put his hands around her waist and held her at arms' length before she pulled loose and walked backward out of the room. Smiling.

CHAPTER EIGHT

If Charlie thought Gary and Hayely had feelings for one another the day the photographer had come to the garden, it paled in comparison to what he saw when he went into work.

By the time Charlie walked in, Hayely had already dropped off a plate full of peanut butter cookies and brownies in the break room and taken an expedited tour of their corporate headquarters. She jumped shyly from her seat on the corner of Gary's desk when Charlie opened the door.

"Hi," she said. "We got here early today."

Hayely mentally gave herself a swift kick for stating the obvious out of embarrassment. Could anyone sense the change between them? She glanced quickly at Gary, scanning for some hint from him and couldn't see anything specific that would give them away. She wasn't sure what she was worried about. After all, it had only been a kiss.

Charlie looked at Gary, thinking that his friend had traveled back ten years into his youth overnight. "So I see."

"Well," Hayely pressed, "how was the big date with Carla?" She was caught between her own personal elation and wanting to hear his news.

Charlie smiled brightly, his eyes fairly glowing. "She's really great. We had the best time together. So," he said deliberately changing the subject, "what do you think of our humble workplace?"

"It's huge. I'd imagined you and Gary sitting on cardboard boxes with plywood for desks. I thought I'd see nails all over the floors, hardhats on the walls and a telephone covered with greasy fingerprints. Nothing like this."

Charlie smiled. He still suspected that Hayely didn't fully comprehend exactly who Gary was or the extent of his empire. How could she? She hadn't been exposed fully to Gary's world yet. Truth was, they had existed much the way she described when Gary first started the business a decade before. But as revenue crept up high into the millions and was now nearly past that, the headquarters had gradually transformed out of necessity into a shining, modern office building.

Gary rested his hand on Hayely's knee as if it belonged there permanently. "We take up the biggest skyscraper in town now. It's amazing. And you should see our other offices. I designed most of them myself and even helped build a couple of them with my own two hands. That's the best. And that's why Charlie here is so amazing. While I'm out playing in the dirt, he keeps things running right here. That's a luxury few company owners can afford these days."

Hayely couldn't imagine she had ever truly thought Charlie was just a personal assistant, because she was growing some suspicions after having looked at his big office. "What's your title exactly?"

He ran a hand over his wayward red hair. "I guess it's COO, if you want to get technical."

Hayely laughed. "Typical. I should know by now how you two downplay everything."

The intercom on Gary's desk buzzed an abrupt interruption. "I'll be right out," he answered into the phone and then announced, "The Bellmarks are in the reception area."

Together the three of them strolled down the carpeted halls to greet the couple, dressed impeccably for the occasion. Gone were Mrs. Bellmark's jeans and sweatshirt and in their place was a navy blue suit of obvious quality. Even Mr. Bellmark wore a suit and tie complete with polished black shoes instead of his brown cowboy boots.

"The only time we get to wear these monkey suits is when we visit an office or go to church," they informed Hayely. "And today's the day for business talk."

With Gary's fingers entwined in hers, Hayely took the lead on her second tour of the day. "Can you believe this?" She stopped and opened a door to the break room. "Gary even has a place where his employees can take naps at lunch." The room next to the one that held all the coffee and dough-nuts boasted a row of cots with heavy curtains that could be pulled around for privacy.

Charlie cleared his throat. "I think the benefits are more important than that even. Full medical, dental, vision, three weeks of vacation per year. Oh, and after every five years of service, Gary sends employees on a paid, three-month sabbatical."

"Generous, my boy," Mr. Bellmark ac-knowledged with a nod. "I've taught you well." He gave a merry wink up at the much larger man.

Hayely felt Gary tense slightly. She may

have been mentally reliving the previous evening, but Mr. Bellmark's answer about the boy's home, she was certain, was the only thing on Gary's mind at the moment.

Hayely couldn't resist, "He's set up an intern program with scholarships for local kids, too. Ten students get a full ride each year if they're lucky." Gary's grip on her fingers was nearly painful and she squeezed back to let him know it.

"They're bragging," Gary said quietly.

"It's good that those around you show such love and loyalty. Even the receptionist sang your praises when we told her who we were. That tells me much about the man you've become," Mr. Bellmark said as he patted Gary hard on the back. "I think we both know that Hilda and I aren't here at your office to tour the break room pastry selection, though. Think we could go to your office and shut the door behind us for a little while?"

In silence, the five of them made their way down the hall back to Gary's big corner office with its enormous glass view of the city stretched out far below. They gathered around a small, oval table and pulled their chairs up tightly against it. No one said a word until a young woman with a red suit and pleasant smile set a pitcher of water with several clear glasses on the table and closed the door with a click behind her. All at once, everyone around the table exhaled and sat up taller.

"I don't know how to say this, so I'll just get straight to the point, my boy. I'm not going to sell you the children's home." Mr. Bellmark drew in a ragged breath and poured himself a shaky glass of water.

Hayely watched Gary's face as the words slowly registered their grim meaning. Though he didn't move a muscle, it seemed to her that some spark of life drained from his expression. More even than her own hurt, she hated to sense his. Arrogance and unsociable behavior she could handle — but not Gary's pain, never that. He didn't deserve it.

"But why?" she asked firmly when no one else spoke.

Gary simply sat at the table and watched the Bellmarks with a piercing stare, awaiting the answer to his wife's question.

Mr. Bellmark met Gary's eyes squarely. "Because you made a promise to me as a boy that only your pride forced you to keep all these years. We honestly hoped you'd forget it one day, but you never did. So, I release you from that promise, son. It's one I don't wish for you to keep."

Gary's straight nose flared slightly. "But I wish to keep it. It's the thing that drove me all these years."

"Listen to me. And really hear me this time. It's too great a burden, and one that you should have never placed on your shoulders. Think for a moment why you wish to keep it. Think and tell me."

Gary sat silent for a minute and answered, "First because I made a vow —"

"— and I've released you from it, so that can no longer be a factor. Next reason."

"Second, I want to pass on what you taught me. I want to give those kids the chances I had or even greater chances. It's a matter of honor." He was relying strictly on his business-bred negotiation skills. His emotions were too twisted around Mr. Bellmark's answer to do otherwise reasonably.

Mr. Bellmark smiled sadly. "But don't you see? You're already doing just that. You don't need to buy our old children's home. You've set up scholarships. And whatever nonsense I taught you, I'm sure you'll teach to your children in turn. Nothing you were given will be lost. You honor us just by doing what you are now — by being Gary Tarleton."

Charlie found his voice. "If this was your intent all along — I mean, if you never wanted to let Gary buy our old home from you, then why did you infer it? Why did you let us think that you would?"

"I don't understand, Charles." The old man took a long sip of water to clear his dry throat. "I did no such thing."

"You did. You said Gary could buy it if he were in the position to. If he made a stable home life for himself and was a family man. You hinted at those things broadly. Hell, it was more than hinting."

Mrs. Bellmark nodded in sudden understanding. "No swearing, Charles," she warned. "I know what you mean now. Though I'll admit, I didn't at first. You all misunderstand. Yes, we wanted desperately for Gary to marry. We didn't want to see him grow old with only his work as a companion. We wanted nothing less than the greatest love for him and for a stable marriage full of laughter and children. By the way, it's no less than we want for you, Charles."

"Well of course we said Gary needed those things," Mr. Bellmark added, "and it may have been in a discussion just before the topic shifted back to where Gary usually shifted it. But those words had nothing whatsoever to do with the home. They had everything to do with his happiness. All we ever wanted was for him to be a happy, honorable person."

Mrs. Bellmark said to Hayely, "Now really, can you imagine being happy separated half the time with Gary traveling to Maine every week to oversee one thing or another there." She turned her gaze back to Gary. "You would be divided between two things and would end up doing neither very well, I'm afraid. You would always have one eye on your past and never both on all the possibilities ahead of you."

Gary's head spun as he thought back years in the past to recall the conversations he'd had about the home. Had he been so intent on the boys' home and the promise of a ten-year-old boy that he hadn't really heard the lesson they were trying to teach him even then?

"But you said you'd rather see it burned to the ground than see the state take it over," Gary said quietly. "Or something to that effect."

"That was a long, long time ago, Gary. Options were fewer back then. With your help, I'm hoping to do something a little different."

"You want me to light the match?" he said dismally.

Mr. Bellmark set down his water glass. "I'm not certain, but I think I want to set up a nonprofit organization, but I'm not even sure how. That nice couple you mentioned before and some experts I plan to steal from some state-run programs can operate it locally. Of course, you and I will have veto power over any decisions they botch. We just won't be involved day-to-day. What do you think?"

Gary wanted to grab something hard and crumble it in his fist. He'd lived under the weight of that promise for so many years that he wasn't sure how to live otherwise. He'd tailored his entire existence around the day — this day — when he would sit with Mr. Bellmark and take up the torch. He looked numbly at Hayely, not sure what to do for the first time in his life. This must be how Hayely felt all those times she talked about finding a career, he thought.

"I've wasted everything," Gary said. "My entire life wasted chasing something that didn't exist."

Mrs. Bellmark looked at him sternly. "No. You were chasing something before the idea to buy the home ever entered your mind. If it weren't that, it would have been something else you'd have fought for."

Hayely looked from face to face and set her hand delicately over Gary's on top of the table. She knew reason when she heard it and she understood how sometimes wishes were refused out of kindness.

"I think they're making sense. You need to let the ten-year-old orphan and his promise go," Hayely said in a near whisper.

"Really?" His hazel eyes looked intently into her glassy ones. "Really?" he repeated.

She nodded. "I really don't think your plan has changed much when you think about it. You can still repair that church down the road. You can still set up more scholarships for the boys there."

"That's true," Gary agreed.

"And," Hayely continued, "the couple you wanted to run it will be running it after all. The Bellmarks have just made sure you'll be at home starting a family someday — your own brand new children's home here in Nevada, so to speak."

Gary let out a huge breath that shook his big shoulders. After holding so tightly for so many years to what seemed to be the most important business deal of his life, he felt strangely calm that it hadn't come to pass. For once, there were no fears of instability, no misplaced vows to drive him. All he needed to do was run his company and — what exactly did he need to do with Hayely?

"Wow," he said with a laugh. "How did I get all this? I have everything I wanted after all. And I didn't even see it coming." Then a fearful thought came to him. If he hadn't been so driven, so stubborn — if one single event had been altered in his life along the way, he might never have found Hayely Black signing a paper that made her Hayely Tarleton. He would have never even known her. That concept suddenly chilled him more than the change in plans for the children's home.

Mrs. Bellmark let out a sigh of relief. "We were so worried about how you might take our news. We hoped you would understand."

All at once, everyone rose from the table and went from one person to the next with hugs and kisses. There was more laughter than Hayely had heard in years, and again she noticed a light creeping back into Gary's face.

With words of regret, the Bellmarks had to leave for the airport at last. They couldn't stay later; the flight to Maine was a long one and a taxi already awaited them in the parking lot below. All too quickly, the lively gathering narrowed down to only two as Charlie also left to pick up Carla for a lunch date. When Gary and Hayely at last sat alone and exhausted in his office, they simply looked outside at the view.

Hayely stretched out on Gary's leather

executive sofa while he leaned back in his chair and kicked his feet up onto his desk.

"Are you alright?"

"I am," he answered. "You know, I'm not going to work weekends anymore. I've worked them my whole life. I'm just not going to do that anymore." He put his hands behind his neck and watched an airplane with its hundreds of passengers sail by noiselessly in the distant blue sky.

"A lighter workload would be good," she said as softly as possible. "You'd have more time for a personal life."

"What do you want to do during the day after all the interior design is done? It almost is, you know. I could set up something for you here?"

Lord above, was she still an employee first and foremost to him? She frowned and would have thrown a pillow at his head if she'd had more than one with her on the sofa.

"I want to do something for myself, thank you very much. I just don't know what it is yet," she said at length.

Gary's eyes followed the trail of the plane. "If you could fly away anywhere right now, where would it be?"

"Way to change the subject. Don't you think dinner and a movie would be a better place to start getting to know each other better?"

"We've already done dinner. Several times." His voice grew low and gentle as he looked at her.

Hayely spun around on her bottom on the slick sofa and sat up straight. Frustrating, that's what he was. "Okay. I'll play. I've always wanted to see Pompeii."

"You want to see a bunch of dead people covered in ash?"

"Not the most romantic?"

"Nope." He shook his head. "How about a safari in Africa? We could sleep in tents under the stars."

We? She pondered the idea. "I'm not big on sunburns or being lion bait. You'll have to do better than that."

He laughed in defeat. "It's settled then. For our fantasy trip, Italy it is, all the way to Pompeii. For now, want to come down with me to one of the sites? I'll introduce you to the crew."

"You know, I think I'd rather just go back to the house. I'm a little tired of make-believe and fantasy."

"You want something real?" He leaned in close, so close she could feel the heat of his body warming her.

"Real?" She pressed her hands against his

chest. "Try having to figure out how to tell my parents that I went and got married months ago and couldn't seem to find the time to tell them. Doesn't get much more real than that."

"You know that's not what I meant," he said.

She lowered her eyes. "What exactly did you mean, Gary?"

He leaned away from her when the answer wouldn't come. He ran his hand across his chin. The right words just wouldn't come when he needed them.

"Do you want me to talk to them?" he finally offered.

Hayely sighed when he sidestepped the loaded question.

"Maybe I should just tell them I'm married but it's only a business deal, that I sold myself to pay for a watch."

Gary grimaced visibly. "Look, I —"

She put her hand up as if to stop his words. "Or maybe you could just kiss me," she whispered.

As he pulled her into his arms, all Hayely could think was that the Bellmarks were gone and there was really no more need for the charade. And soon all the painting would be finished. The fairy tale was ending just as soon as it started, and she was half scared and half filled with hope to think where reality might lead.

CHAPTER NINE

A day or two passed while Hayely summoned the courage to call her family. She felt slightly sick to her stomach that morning and it didn't help that when she dialed her parents' phone number off and on all morning, she connected with nothing but an annoying answering machine on the other end.

A gnawing anxiety twirled around inside her. All but once in her life, her father's decisions had somehow wound up being hers. Then she'd taken a stand against him and it had nearly severed their relationship entirely. Her decision had taken her across the country to Nevada and now into . . . this.

"Time to stand on your own two feet and be an adult, Hayely," she whispered to herself. "And live with your own decisions." She stared at the telephone and hoped it would ring in spite of the tense conversation she knew would follow.

Her interior design duties for the mansion were finished for the most part, and she'd be moving out soon. She'd hoped Gary might say something — anything. But the fact was, she'd scarcely seen him alone since the Bellmarks left. He seemed distant and deep in thought, yet he still hadn't explained what he'd meant by "something real."

Dressed in sweatpants and a color-splattered shirt, Hayely finished painting the last unfinished room that morning. The place was definitely opposite what it had been only a few months before. The light from the stained glass windows fell on ferns and plants with dark green leaves. Candles, chandeliers, and firelight bathed the living room whenever possible, and the richly colored walls and decadent fabrics had turned the cold marble and stone into a haven of comfort.

Hayely dropped her brush back into the near-empty paint bucket when she heard Gary coming down the hall to find her. She'd seen a lightness come over him since his meeting with the Bellmarks. She still had to nudge him to get him to speak nicely to anyone he didn't know well, but she had to admit that she'd even grown to enjoy his standoffish qualities. Now she knew it; when she moved out, his loss would cut.

His lush voice rolled toward her before she saw him. "Hayely, the strangest thing happened this morning." He walked around the corner and leaned in the doorway with his loose jeans shifting in just the right places. "I tried to call the lawyer's office and get our file back from them today."

"Why?"

"I thought we could shred all the copies of that ridiculous contract into a thousand pieces together."

"I would love that. So what was strange?" She pushed a strand of hair back. How she'd gotten paint the color of tomato soup in it, she could only imagine.

"Their office was broken into last week. The only thing stolen was our file."

Hayely set the paint bucket down on the floor and her hand fluttered up to rest over her heart. "Are you sure it isn't just missing? Misfiled?"

Gary crossed his denim-covered arms over his chest, looking sterner that ever. "Gone. Stolen." He paused for a moment. "Can you think of anyone who would have known I used that particular lawyer to draw up our agreement?"

Hayely sank down into a nearby chair and didn't even seem to notice as the white drop cloth slid off and bunched around her. I'm going to fire some idiot today. I just don't know who yet. Maybe it'll be someone who receives personal deliveries on company time.

"Oh no," she whispered and then looked up at Gary's piercing hazel eyes. "The courier. You had the package sent to me at the office and it had a label from your lawyer's office on it."

"Who saw that package?"

Hayely's grey eyes hardened. "Kathy."

Gary's jaw clenched and unclenched. "I'm tired of dealing with that witch. She's gone past unethical and flown on her broomstick straight into illegal. I ought to turn her in to the police."

"How could you prove it? You know she probably didn't break into the office herself anyway. She probably planted the seed in what's his name — Darryl's head and had him do it after an all-night bender anyway."

Gary struck his hand in anger against the doorframe. "She can't use it. If she tries, I'll have her bony behind tossed behind bars so fast —"

The melodious chimes of the doorbell sang through the house and interrupted Gary's sentence. "Don't tell me Charlie forgot his keys again," he muttered with eyes still furious and filled with a livid glint.

He turned and stomped toward the entry-way with Hayely following on his heels.

Gary turned the bolt on the door and as he did, yelled out, "You don't have to keeping ringing the thing. We heard you." With a final twist, he flung open the door as wide as it would go.

Hayely jumped back as Gary moved almost casually away from the impact of the heavy door. With his arm stretched high against the side of the wood, he said to her, "I think it's for you."

All at once a tight red fist appeared in the house from whoever stood outside, and it was aimed at Gary's stomach through the open door. He stepped back just in time to avoid the blow.

"What have you done to my daughter?" A pair of flashing grey eyes that looked much like Hayely's glared up at Gary.

Gary looked down at the shorter, stockier man on his doorstep. His visitor was round-faced and determined as the sunlight bounced off his nearly bald head. He still had both of his reddened hands clenched tightly at his sides, a bunch of papers clutched in the one he hadn't swung at Gary.

Gary hadn't noticed the slender woman

standing there next to her husband at first. She was about the same height as her daughter, but seemed so thoroughly engrossed in the pavement at her feet that Gary couldn't yet see the similarities in her face.

"Mr. and Mrs. Black," he said with confidence. "Come in."

"I most certainly will not," Hayely's father declared with a great huff. "I've come to take my daughter back home with us and away from you — you, scoundrel!" he shouted and shook the wad of papers in Gary's face. "I know what you've done to her. I've read all about it."

Mrs. Black rushed in between them when she saw Hayely emerge from behind Gary. "Oh, my baby girl. What has this horrible man done to you? You look awful. Did he kidnap you and force you to sign that horrible document? I know he must have done something terrible for you to have signed it."

"It's nothing better than slave labor," Mr. Black roared. "We'll see justice done here. I don't care who you think you are, Gary Tarleton. You can't buy people."

Hayely's mother touched her daughter's paint-globbed hair and looked sadly at her ragged clothes. "Look how thin she is. And her hair." Tears sprung to the woman's eyes. "She hasn't been treated right at all. It was just as we feared. Come, Hayely. We'll take you home with us right this minute."

Hayely pushed her mother's hand away. "You don't understand at all. You have no idea what you're talking about. I tried to call." Her voice was softer than she wanted it to be, slipping back into the genteel demeanor her father had instilled in her.

Mr. Black pushed his way past Gary and shook the papers again. "We understand everything. It's all right here in this legal document."

Gary slammed the door shut and startled them all. Drawing himself up to his full height, he pointed to the living room and commanded, "Go in there and sit. Now."

For a moment Hayely thought her mother was going to faint on the spot and her father was going to take another swing at Gary's midsection. "Let's go sit down," she soothed. "I'll make us all some coffee and we'll work this out."

Gary strode into the living room and took his seat. His rigid posture told Hayely he just might have reached his already short limit on politeness for the day. He actually seemed angry, and not just because of the stolen documents.

"You can sit together there on the sofa. I picked out the furniture myself," she said and then left the room to fetch the coffee. Here it comes, she told herself. The worst possible scenario I could have imagined. At least there was no doubt what Kathy Mark had done with the stolen agreement.

When she set the coffee down in front of her parents and Gary, it was obvious none of them had spoken a word while she was out of the room. Gary had relaxed somewhat and now looked positively unruffled, slightly curious, and yet a bit hostile. Her mother ran her hand down the smooth fabric of the sofa while her father's face faded down through several lesser shades of red.

Hayely sat down in the chair nearest Gary. "You need to know that the person who sent you that document is no friend of mine. She did it just to cause trouble."

"Are you saying it's a fake?" her father questioned.

Hayely looked down. "No, it's real."

"Then pack your bags. We're taking you out of here." He threatened to stand until Hayely gestured for him to sit.

"I'll be moving out of here soon anyway. You read the agreement."

For a moment, Hayely looked around the

room at her mother, then her father and finally Gary. Each beat of her heart thudded in her ears. She could go back to the East Coast. She could go back to school and never have to work in an office as an executive assistant again. She'd have the chance to meet the kind of man her family admired, the kind who would marry her and become the father of her children. All she had to do was compromise. The time of reckoning was at hand.

Then she saw the emotion swirl and hazel colors flash in Gary's eyes. His hands clenched tightly into fists. He was waiting to hear her answer with an intensity that made her heart thud even louder.

"I'm not leaving with you," she said firmly. Calmly.

"I don't think I heard what I think I heard," her father said.

She raised her chin and met her father's gaze. "I didn't want it to be like this. How did you get here so soon anyway?"

"So soon," her mother sobbed. "My only daughter has a wedding and is married half a year, and that's too soon for us to talk to her about it." She blew her nose into a pristine handkerchief.

"It wasn't a wedding," Mr. Black corrected. "It was an entrance into indentured servitude."

Gary leaned forward. She wasn't leaving him. She'd given her answer, the one he'd wanted to ask her himself and had stopped short of a dozen times in the past two days. He'd told her before that he didn't let go of things he cared for. He meant to prove it now.

A hardened twinkle of amusement also lurked in his eyes. He'd watched his new in-laws for several minutes now, and it didn't seem to him that they were out to hurt Hayely — just the opposite. Only parents who really cared about a child would jump on the first plane, cross the United States and arrive hopping mad on his doorstep to rescue her.

Mrs. Black dabbed at her nose and sniffled loudly.

Gary sat back again, reached out to rest his hand on Hayely's knee and then thought the better of it.

"Why don't you tell them what happened? The whole truth of it," Gary suggested.

"Well," she started, "I was walking across the parking lot with too many packages and I ran into Gary." She sipped her coffee and continued. "I mean I literally ran into him.

And in the process, I obliterated a very expensive gift he'd just bought for his best friend, Charlie."

"That would account for the twelve-thousand-dollar figure I read in this contract with the devil," her father stated and slapped the papers against his sturdy leg for emphasis.

"Yes. That was what it was worth," she agreed quietly. "And I wanted to do the honorable thing and repay the debt, so I agreed to Gary's terms. I wasn't going to tell anyone, I was just going to set things right, do as he asked and move on with my life."

Her mother turned white. "He didn't force you to — to — did he?"

"Mother! He didn't force me to do anything. It started out as a business arrangement like I said, but then we —" She slammed down her coffee mug. "Mom, I ended up feeling something, feelings that I shouldn't feel. It isn't professional, I know. The six months is over, but when he kissed me —"

"I don't believe it," Mr. Black sputtered. "No man treats my daughter like, like — I can't even think of a word for it. And no decent father would let his only daughter throw away her life. Hells bells. If you even stay on as his employee, we'll disinherit you. That's what we'll do. And we'll turn your shrine of a bedroom in a study."

Gary said curtly, "You don't mean that." He recognized a bluff when he heard it, but suspected Hayely was too emotionally close to the situation to notice.

The man shook his head in resignation, "No. I don't. We're just trying to do right by our Hayely."

"Believe me, so am I," Gary said. "There's nothing more important to me."

Mr. Black looked at his new son-in-law with piqued interest. He was glad he hadn't been able to punch him at the front door after all — his hand would still be hurting if he had. And now he thought he understood another meaning in Gary's simple sentence and earnest demeanor. He could see it in the man's eyes. Could it be that one of the wealthiest, most widely known men in the country had fallen in love with his daughter?

"So," Hayely continued with a stronger voice. "We spent time together and we have similar values and ideas, plans . . . I don't know how this will end for us, but I need to be here to find out."

Mr. Black turned to Gary. "You have more money than all the gods on Olympus and could take your pick of women. Why her?"

The two men looked at each other in silent understanding.

"Thanks a lot, Dad," Hayely murmured.

Gary shrugged. "At first? Because she didn't know who I was."

Mr. Black shook his round head from side to side and chuckled loudly. "Now that I can believe. Our Hayely never paid any attention to money."

"It's wonderful, isn't it?" Gary said with a grin. "She looks straight through to the person and doesn't even notice his bankbook."

Mr. Black slapped his thigh and laughed. "You should have seen how she reacted when we tried to get her to date one of the boys down the road. She said he was a 'stuck-up blueblood' and kept hiding in the bathroom to avoid him. A simple 'no' would have sufficed. I can tell you're a good man, Tarleton. I won't object to her staying here if you make it honorable."

Hayely had sat silent long enough while everyone around her talked about her as if she didn't exist. They were trying to make her decisions for her again and finally the anger welled up in her. She stood up straight, nearly sloshing the coffee over the rim of her cup.

"You won't object? Ha! I'm not going

back with you," she declared, "partly because I'm sick of everyone trying to protect me to death. I'm staying in Nevada. And it was my decision."

Gary gave a little wink. "I might have a little something to do with it, too."

Hayely's father walked over to her and caught her up in his pudgy arms. He was more than sure of Gary's intentions by now. Anyone could see how much he treasured Hayely.

"You mother always tells me I'm too abrupt, too brusque. I don't mean to be."

"You don't?" Hayely asked her father. She felt dazed, unsure she'd even spoken.

"No. There's a chance I went overboard trying to make sure you were happy," her father added. "I shouldn't have worried."

Gary reached out, took her by the hand and gently pulled her down to rest of the arm of his chair. "Don't be too angry with them. It's just that they love you as much as I do."

Hayely breathed in and out quickly while her head still tried to wrap itself around what Gary had said. He loved her? She loved him! She'd danced around the word for weeks and pressed it from her mind whenever it had threatened to surface there. She felt shivers through her body whenever he looked her way. With a touch he could soothe or ignite her. She loved his family values, loved his gruffness, loved the construction dust on his clothes . . .

Gary took her by the hands and looked into her eyes. "Well? What do you say we forget about the deal and the divorce we'd have to get?"

She nodded. "Say it again."

"I fell in love with you and you're not leaving me."

"I love you, too," she whispered.

Mrs. Black broke down fully into tears as she fully absorbed the truth. "You know what this means, don't you? I've missed my only daughter's wedding." Big wet tears rolled down cheekbones that called Hayely's own to mind.

Hayely turned to Gary. "Then we'll have to create memories they haven't missed. Babies. Celebrations of anniversaries and old photo albums filled with our life together."

Gary placed his hands on her arms. "Look at me, Hayely. Look up at me. Let's start now."

They all followed Gary as he went straight to the den, ran over to his desk, flung open the middle drawer and dug furiously through the mass of papers stuffed inside.

As last he grabbed the document he'd been looking for and held it up high in triumph.

"Do you recognize this?"

Hayely looked at the six-month contract she'd signed in the parking lot so many weeks ago. The bright blue ink scrawled along the bottom was unmistakable.

"It's our agreement. I didn't let the lawyer hold the original. I plan on keeping the marriage certificate intact and legal if you'll let me?"

Hayely nodded as if in a trance.

Gary caught the pages by their corners and pulled. When the thick cotton paper tore diagonally in half, he picked up those pieces and shredded them again and again. Soon all that remained was a pile of large confetti, which he swept with a great show of determination into the wastebasket.

"And me without my camera," Hayely said with a laugh that abruptly faded. She looked up at Gary and an expression of sudden knowing came upon her. She hopped up and down once as her elegant fingers flew to her mouth.

"I know what I'm going to do," she breathed out. "I've decided — for a career, I mean." She tucked her chocolate-brown hair back behind her ears in excitement.

Her mother waved a narrow hand in the

air. "It's interior design, isn't it? You've always had such good taste."

Gary struck out his chest and that confidently arrogant expression that drove Hayely crazy showed on his face. "No. She's going to be a chef. Run her own gourmet dessert shop. Cheesecakes and cream puffs."

"She can cook?" Hayely's father asked in wonder. "When did that happen?"

It was Hayely's turn to be smug. "I'm not doing either of those things. But I'm not going to tell any of you busybodies just yet. I've got a few details to work out in my head first." She smiled so that it shined all the way into her eyes. Finally, finally she knew what she wanted to do and she would have Gary at her side through every step.

Gary slid his arm around her waist and whispered, "You'll tell me later, right?" All he got was a gentle elbow to the ribs in response.

The clattering noise of shoes in the marble foyer stopped their conversation. "Charlie has a key," Gary explained. "We're in the den," he yelled out.

Charlie nearly sprinted across the floor, out of breath and visibly agitated as he held on to Carla's hand. She'd smoothed down her spiky black hair into a slick, short bob and it suited her. With an awkward smile

213

and seriousness in her eyes, she gave an ill-at-ease wave to Hayely. Judging from the atmosphere of the room she'd just walked into, they'd stepped into the middle of something important and interrupted it but good. In fact everyone, even Gary, looked as if they had either just finished crying or were about to start.

"You're never going to believe what Carla just heard," Charlie announced, and then noticed Mr. and Mrs. Black in the room.

"These are my parents," Hayely introduced and wiped a remaining tear away. "And this is Charlie, and his girlfriend, Carla."

Gary spoke directly to his friend, "Say whatever it is. They know everything now. We all finally do."

"That Mark woman has a copy of your agreement," Charlie announced with a high level of stress in his voice.

Gary took the wrinkled papers from Mr. Black's hand and held them up. "You mean these?"

Carla nodded. "It looked the same. She has a copy just like that."

Charlie stood behind his new girlfriend and rubbed her shoulders nervously. "Tell them how you saw it. They won't believe it."

Carla moved into the den to sit down and everyone gathered into a circle, standing or sitting closely around her to catch every word.

"Well, I walked over to the mall to get one of those fruit smoothies for lunch. I was sitting at one of those little tables in the food court when I heard somebody behind me say the name Tarleton. Pretty much caught my attention."

"Could you see who it was?" Hayely asked.

"Oh, sure. From a foot or two away. When they were getting ready to leave, I stood up and walked past them to get a good look."

"Go on, Carla," Gary urged. "What else did they say?"

Carla flushed red for a moment. She could hardly believe she was seeing the inside of Gary Tarleton's house, much less sitting on some plush furniture in the middle of his den.

She blinked widely a couple times to collect herself. It was almost comical thinking back at how she and her friends had discussed Gary Tarleton all these years. They hadn't known what they were talking about.

Carla said at length, "It was a woman and some guy talking together. She looked totally out of place dressed up the way she was in the mall. To the hilt. She was telling the guy that she could give him the biggest scoop of his career. Then he said something that gave me the idea he was from that trashy TV show, you know the one, that gossip program?"

Gary nodded, "I know the one."

"That's when I really started to pay attention to him. Then the woman said that you and Hayely hadn't really been married at all — not for real anyway. She said if he put a story about it on television tomorrow evening, she could back it up for him. You know, she would actually prove it when he tries to go for a follow-up story the next day.

"Of course, she'd be an anonymous source. She told him that since nobody wanted you, you'd gone out and bought yourself a bride. She said something about you coming on to her daughter or something and being refused. Then she talked about how Hayely was an incompetent secretary who was going to be fired, so she basically sold her body to pay the bills."

Mr. Black's face had resumed its former shade of scarlet. "Tell me who this devil woman is."

Carla continued, "I'm pretty sure her name is Kathy Mark. She's been in the store a few times since the Chamber of Commerce Banquet. None of us likes her, so we don't say anything, but she's always trying to steer the conversation around to Hayely. Never buys anything either. I saw her clear as day when I got up and walked out of the food court. She stayed for a little while after the reporter left and was reading a document. It looked just like that one." She pointed to the papers Gary had held up. "I could even see your names on it and the lawyer's letterhead."

"Which reporter was it, do you know?" Gary asked.

"Sure. I'd know that guy's voice anywhere. Mel Reilly. His show comes on at eight."

"Do you think she ever showed him the document or gave him a copy?"

Carla shook her head. "I don't think so. I mean, not from their conversation and she only took out the papers and started reading them after he'd gotten up and walked away."

"You're wonderful, Carla. We owe you one." Gary squeezed Hayely's hand. "I'm heading down to the TV station."

"How do you plan on stopping them from airing such garbage?" So much had happened in the span of fifteen minutes that she was still trying to wrap her mind around it all.

Gary gave a crooked grin. "If you had to choose between an exclusive interview with a man who never gives interviews, or a shaky story that will promise him a multi-million-dollar defamation of character suit, which would you choose?"

Charlie nodded enthusiastically. "Good thinking. I think I'll pay a visit to Ms. Mark. Hey, did she ever send your final paycheck? I shouldn't have made that comment to her at the banquet. Probably made her dig in her heels."

Hayely shook her head. "No, there's been nothing in the mail. I called and asked the payroll department where it was, but didn't get anywhere. They were really uncomfortable."

"That's completely illegal." Mr. Black drew himself up to full stature. "I'll go along with this young man and we'll deal with that foul woman once and for all."

Hayely looked around the room and found that all the bravado tickled her. A few months ago, she was sure she would have been frustrated and not just a little angry with all these men jumping to her rescue.

The less mature, less secure Hayely would have assumed they were trying to control her and didn't trust in her own strength. *Sometimes I think you mistake acts of caring for disrespect.* She sensed nothing but caring around her, and she also sensed Gary waiting to see if she'd give her usual prickly reaction or not.

"No," she said with a great deal of calm firmness. "I'm going down to K. L. Mark Enterprises and handling this myself. All of it. I won't get personal. I won't tell her off. I'll just get my paycheck and let her know we're aware she has our stolen agreement."

"You sure you don't need backup?" Charlie asked.

"Thanks, but no. I need to do this. I'm closing one chapter and opening up a new one." She caught Gary's gaze and held it after he gave her a quick kiss. "I'm going to change clothes and head over there right now. I'll meet you all at eight o'clock in front of the TV."

Charlie smiled broadly as he took in all the kissing and hand holding. "So you two finally admitted you're in love?"

Hayely's dad answered, "You bet your bottom they have."

In spite of disastrous story that threatened them, Hayely had never been happier. She could hardly stand herself she was so filled with joy.

CHAPTER TEN

Hayely sped down the highway with the top of her shiny silver car down to let the golden rays of sunlight in. With her smooth grey slacks, lightly woven springtime sweater the same shade of red as the leather interior and her sunglasses with red lenses, it almost looked as if she'd dressed to match the car.

She tied a long light grey scarf around her neck and laughed as the wind twirled it back across the seat. Those times when she had felt so miserable? They hardly seemed worth remembering now that she had grown so far past that emotion. She would have a real husband in Gary and an amazing career plan in mind. She smiled to herself and wondered when she might decide to let everyone else in on her ideas.

For months, whenever she'd gone shopping, she'd ended up designing outfits of her own, giving her sketches to Carla, and then having the boutique's tailor actually sew the clothing for her. What she'd learned was not only that she enjoyed the creative process, but she was good at it!

Her taste in fabrics and colors were always dead on, and her original styles were such that she couldn't find similar in stores. And what was even better — she could design the patterns at home while raising children and experimenting in the kitchen. She'd even been toying with the idea of hiring Carla on to manage a new boutique filled with the Hayely line — but she'd have to give that and her brand name some more thought before saying anything.

Along with her husband and career, Hayely had also discovered a newfound confidence that just might let her stand up for herself with some measure of class. If she could handle Kathy Mark with dignity, she was sure she'd be able to withstand worse with even greater grace from here on out. She was well on the way to understanding her father, too. She had only one more thing to accomplish, and she'd have that done in only a few more anxious minutes.

She turned her car into the big parking lot, stepped out onto the pavement and bumped the door shut with her hip just for fun. She'd done that the day she met Gary and it seemed fitting to do it again on the last day she'd ever have to make the long walk up to that dreaded office.

With her grey leather boots clicking along the pavement, she walked with her head held high past the fine jewelry store, past the gift shop, past the deli and pushed the button on the elevator. She was a woman going to the office with a mission — her own this time.

When Hayely stepped into K. L. Mark's reception area, the office fell silent around her. Half the employees she saw in the background were complete strangers to her, but some remained who recognized her and with them the shock was instant and visible. There was also another new and very friendly receptionist to greet her, she noticed.

And she had to admit, there were butterflies zipping around inside her stomach so the receptionist's warm smile helped. Be strong, Hayely thought. Don't shrink away this time. Stand firm. Have integrity, though. Don't act like her. No cussing and no yelling.

When she gave her name and asked for Kathy, the receptionist dutifully called back to her former boss's office, giving away the fact that the woman was there. Hayely imagined that single action would cost the receptionist her job. From the stricken look on her face as she listened to the voice on the other end of the line, Hayely would bet money on it.

"You can go back," the receptionist whispered and fought to hold back tears. "I've never been called that name before."

Hayely quickly scribbled her cell phone number down on a notepad. "If you wind up needing a new job, call me here. I've been in your shoes and can help."

Kathy's door was wide open when Hayely approached it.

Kathy Mark sat behind her desk and observed Hayely with absolute hatred in her faded blue eyes. "What the hell do you want? Do I need to have someone escort you out of the building?"

"I came for my final paycheck," Hayely said with more composure than she felt. She'd come this far — no time to turn back now. "By law, it was due to me weeks ago, and I understand it hasn't been issued yet."

"Maybe it's lost in the mail." Kathy gave a mean little smile and tapped her fingertips together in front of her. Hayely remembered an article in which Kathy had been described as ruthless and how she had gloated about that term for days. Did she actually take a reputation for hurting people as a compliment?

Hayely ignored her snide comment and continued with her mission. It was coming easier with each sentence. "I've spoken with Payroll several times now. If the check isn't in my hands when I leave here, I'll be filing charges with the appropriate state agencies and taking you to court." Her statement came out plainly, flatly — and just the way she planned it without her voice increasing even a decibel.

"If that's the way you want to play it, sweetie."

Hayely fought the urge to throw something pointy at Kathy, but then pity took over. With all the blessings she'd been given, it was hard for her to envision how horrible it would be to live in Kathy Mark's position. All the woman's soul strove for was physical appearance and dollar signs — there was little more to her and little goodness created around her. She knew Kathy believed she was to be envied, but Hayely thought maybe when the woman was alone at home during the evenings the sadness of her situation crept over her privately.

"That's the way it will be, Kathy," she countered softly. "I don't want to have to do that because a trial will expose all your personal issues — Darryl or Dee's personal issues to the community. I don't want to sink to that and I hope you won't force me to."

Kathy pounded her fist down on her desktop. "I will not have this discussion," she bellowed. "You've had problems, too. Lots of problems in your past." Her eyes narrowed to slits accented by short pale lashes. Her face suddenly looked old — very old and very hard.

Hayely heard the hum of distant discussions stop and silence fall in the carpeted halls outside Kathy's office. She knew that just in the way people always overheard Kathy mistreating people, they were now overhearing this conversation. And she recognized a desperate attempt to dig up dirt when she heard it.

"Nice try. But, no — I haven't had any problems," Hayely said coolly and brushed the ludicrous accusation aside. "It's also come to my attention that Mel Reilly may be airing a story of interest to you tonight. You might want to watch it."

An uncertain flicker passed across Kathy's anger-contorted face. She pulled her teal tweed jacket tighter around herself and crossed her legs.

Hayely continued in hushed tones to avoid the office eavesdroppers, "Did you know

Gary's lawyer's office was broken into recently? Seems the only thing missing was a document of ours."

"Don't you dare try to accuse me of anything. I'll run you out of town on a rail."

Hayely couldn't even bring herself to smile. She knew the rail construction project K. L. Mark had been involved in recently had its funding turned down by the local voters. Kathy's words were sadly ironic and futile.

"I just wanted you to know that the lawyer filed a police report. Anyone found with their hands on that document would run into some serious trouble with the law."

"This meeting is over." Kathy made a great show of trying to regain power of the room. She stormed by and put her hand on the edge of the open door. Hayely remembered reading about just that meeting-ending technique in a second-rate manager's manual, and that knowledge made Kathy's act seem all the more impotent.

Hayely stood firmly where she had been standing all along. "It would be a shame if anything in that document got out — especially with so many people at the mall having seen the woman who stole it sitting there in broad daylight reading it."

"Get out."

Hayely said very quietly, "I want my paycheck and all the copies of that document. If memory serves, you probably have them both in the file cabinet next to the window."

Hayely laughed and pounded her palms against the steering wheel as she drove back toward home. Her paycheck and what she suspected weren't the only copies of her marriage agreement sat under her purse on the floor beside her.

When she got home and walked into the kitchen, she found a note telling her that Charlie and Carla had taken her parents out to dinner. What a relief that she didn't have to cook that night! She couldn't imagine a more unlikely foursome sharing dinner conversation, though. The idea of her father and free-spirited Carla debating current issues actually made her laugh out loud. Then another thought hit her. Home. This really was her home now.

With the house empty, she darted upstairs and turned the gilded handles that released a stream of frothy water into Gary's round black bathtub, which she supposed was also hers to share. She'd have to get used to that thought — and bring in some new towels with "HT" stitched onto their ends.

It looked like Gary had finished hanging pictures, and there was rarely a room to be found in the house that wasn't graced with a portrait of the two of them together. He'd even put a framed picture of them on the counter next to the sumptuous gold bath beads and white fleur-de-lis shaped soaps.

When her bubble bath churned up mountains of white foam, she lit a candle and slid down inside the great marble hollow. With a great sigh, she rested her head back and let all of her cares evaporate into the steam.

"I'm always finding you like this," Gary said softly from the doorway. He held the grey silk scarf she'd dropped on the bedroom floor, and ran it through his fingers. "I can't wait for our company to be gone."

"How did the big interview go?" she asked, her pulse pounding in her throat as she caught his meaning. So he'd been in the house the day of the Banquet after all. She sunk deeper into her bubblebath until she was hidden.

"Controlled the damage before it even started," he murmured down against the back of her head. "How about your visit with Ms. Trash-in-a-suit?"

Hayely couldn't help but smile at his term for her former boss. "Got my paycheck. And three photocopies of our stolen agreement if you can believe that."

"Really? Now that I didn't expect."

"Neither did I. I think you might have to hire another receptionist, though. I probably just cost one her job this morning."

"We'll have to talk about that later." He bent to kiss her.

His touches were growing familiar to her, she realized. There was a comfort and a security in them now.

He set a damp and crumpled newspaper into her hands. "I think it will explain a lot about why that woman was bent on causing trouble." He pointed to the business section.

"K. L. Mark Enterprises closes local offices." She didn't know whether to laugh outright or remain solemn and dignified.

Gary noticed her struggle. "I think it's okay to step off the high road for just a second."

Hayely kept smiling and read out loud, "Kathy Mark, owner of K. L. Mark Enterprises announced the pending closure of that company's offices in Nevada, citing a poor economy and pending relocation of its headquarters. Industry insiders believe recent allegations of falsified credentials and high staff turnover may be partially to blame. Following a series of lawsuits filed by former employees and clients during the past few months, K. L. Mark Enterprises has been unable to secure positions on subcontractor teams —"

"What did I tell you? Instant karma." He smiled and kissed her sweet-smelling hair again.

"You were right. I never doubted it. But, you know, I felt sorry for her today. All I could see when I looked at her was a desperately insecure woman whose lack of values is eating away at her. I wouldn't trade her places for anything."

Gary grimaced. "Perish the thought."

She glanced up at the clock and pushed at him playfully. "We're going to be late. Look at the time. Out, out! I've got to get dressed."

She tied her blue robe around her and when she opened the bedroom door, she could hear the sounds of the TV coming through the surrounding speakers in the upstairs media room, and knew that Charlie and Carla had already arrived with her parents in tow.

"Come on!" She grabbed his hand and pulled him willingly down the hall behind her.

Charlie looked up as they ran into the room. "You made it just in time." He pointed the remote control at the screen just as the introductory music faded.

"Look — there's the little creep right now," Gary said as Mel Reilly's face appeared on the screen. Gary sank heavily with Hayely down into the cushy black theater chairs she had arranged in short lines in front of the big screen. The way she'd lined things out, they'd be holding private movie screenings before he knew it. Was that a movie theater popcorn popper in the corner of the room? He knew instinctively that it was.

Mel Reilly began, "Tonight we're pleased to bring you what no news program has been able to bring you before — an exclusive interview with Nevada's very own self-made multi-millionaire, Gary Tarleton.

"We were shocked earlier today when what we first deemed to be a very credible source brought certain shady allegations to this reporter regarding Mr. Tarleton's marriage. We'll address those allegations tonight in our feature interview."

Segue music rolled through the room. "I just hate the way he emphasizes certain words like some big conspiracy is happening," Carla said with a shake of the head and then they all fell silent.

The camera faded in to show Gary and

Mel Reilly seated opposite one another in a pair of tacky yellow and orange patterned chairs. "Mr. Tarleton. Gary. You don't mind if I call you Gary, do you? I just want to say what an honor it is to have you here with us."

"Thank you," the recorded Gary replied with that firm, quiet look on his face that said he'd already analyzed his interviewer and taken a dislike to him.

"I'll get straight to the point," Mel continued and leaned toward Gary with beady eyes glinting in the hot, overly bright studio lighting. "We have been told that you bought your wife in a sordid business deal more than six months ago and are no longer even married at all. Is this true?"

"No." Gary rested his arms on the sides of his chair and looked confidently at his interviewer. Even seated, he seemed to tower over the other man.

Mel cleared his throat as he learned the hard way not to ask yes-no questions of Gary Tarleton. "Can you explain why these allegations have been made?"

"No."

Mel almost grimaced as he nervously slicked back his heavily moussed, greying hair with the palm of his hand. He'd done it again. "What I mean," he recovered, "is that I'd like you to explain to all our viewers out there what your current marital status is."

"I'm married," Gary answered and to Mel's great relief, continued, "to a wonderful woman named Hayely. I think quite a few people had the chance to meet her at the Chamber Banquet a while back. It's true that we married more than half a year ago and we couldn't be happier together."

"That's wonderful news, Gary. I'm sure we're all very happy for you. But what about these rumors that she's just another hired hand, so to speak?"

"I learned long ago never to listen to rumors," Gary said darkly. "They never tell the whole story. The real truth of the matter is, I met Hayely and hired her to do the interior design work on my new house. We got to know each other and fell in love."

"So there's no truth to the rumors that Hayely is only an employee?"

"Nope."

"So how do you explain your wedding? I understand it was impromptu at best. No friends, no family present to watch the two of you exchanges vows. How do you explain that, Gary?"

He shot the man a dark, serious look that made the reporter nervously clear his throat again. Then Gary paused for a moment before answering, "My thoughtlessness. That's how I would explain it. That's partially why I wanted to do this interview, to make an announcement and redeem myself. I didn't give Hayely a chance to start our marriage with all the trimmings. She deserves so much more than what I gave her. I can't rewind time, but I think I can make up for my impatience."

"Go on, tell us how," Mel almost pleaded. His panicked expression said that if Gary stopped talking, he was afraid he couldn't make him start again.

"I'd like to ask my bride to renew our wedding vows. We'll do it in a big church ceremony full of friends and family, if that's what she wants. The white dress and everything. Cake. Flowers galore. The works." He looked directly into the camera with a twinkle in his hazel eyes. "What do you think, Hayely Tarleton? Marry me all over again?"

Carla and Hayely's mother let out a collective sigh and looked with misty eyes at Hayely. There was even a tear or two lurking in her father's eyes, though he tried his best to look brave. It was clear Gary had taken a potentially nasty situation and was walking away from it looking like the most romantic hero in town.

As Mel did the wrap-up, the off-the-television Gary took the remote control from Charlie's fingers and turned down the volume. He took Hayely's slender hand in his own and asked, "Well? Is that a yes?"

"What do you think?" she answered with a laugh.

"I think you'll do." He suddenly looked her up and down as if surveying merchandise before making a great purchase. He ran a hand through his tousled brown hair and then across his chin, but there was no mistaking the amusement on his face this time.

She fought a smile, but her eyes had already smoked over with emotion. "I'll do what?" She recalled all too well their first meeting and said a silent prayer of thanks. This time, she had no trouble meeting his gaze. In fact, she wanted to spend the rest of her years doing just that.

"Here's the deal. I want a real, permanent wife. I want conversations and plenty of questions. I'll be requiring friendship and silver-eyed children — and more pot roast while I'm at it. Not to mention a companion for the honeymoon to Pompeii I've just booked."

Hayely tucked her hair back behind her

ear and whispered with a smile, "Well then, Mr. Tarleton, I suppose I'll — I do."